the ILLUSTRATED
VERSION *of* THINGS

the ILLUSTRATED
VERSION *of* THINGS

AFFINITY KONAR

FC2
TUSCALOOSA

The University of Alabama Press
Tuscaloosa, Alabama 35487-0380

Published by FC2, an imprint of the University of Alabama Press, with support provided by Florida State University, the Publications Unit of the Department of English at Illinois State University, and the School of Arts and Sciences, University of Houston–Victoria

Address all editorial inquiries to: Fiction Collective Two, University of Houston–Victoria, School of Arts and Sciences, Victoria, TX 77901-5731

⊗

The paper on which this book is printed meets the minimum requirements of American National Standard for Information Sciences—Permanence of Paper for Printed Library Materials, ANSI Z39.48–1984

Library of Congress Cataloging-in-Publication Data
Konar, Affinity.
  The illustrated version of things / by Affinity Konar. — 1st ed.
    p. cm.
  ISBN-13: 978-1-57366-147-8 (pbk. : alk. paper)
  ISBN-10: 1-57366-147-3 (pbk. : alk. paper)
  1. Young women—Fiction. 2. Orphans—Fiction. 3. Mental illness—Fiction. 4. Domestic fiction. I. Title.
  PS3611.O5844I45 2009
  813'.6—dc22

                                2008036711

Book Design: Kenneth Earl and Tara Reeser
Cover Design: Lou Robinson
Typeface: Garamond
Produced and printed in the United States of America

for my MOTHER *and my* FATHER

ACKNOWLEDGMENTS

I am grateful for the support of the David Berg Foundation, whose generosity enabled the writing of this book, and to FC2 for making it more than I ever imagined it could be through the talents of Brenda Mills, Dan Waterman, Tara Reeser, and Carmen Edington. A pronounced measure of my thanks belongs to: Pranav Behari, Lydia Millet, Joyce Polansky, Ben Marcus, Sam Lipsyte, Kate Bernheimer, Ashley Foley, Jonathan Konar, Ricky Cruz, Jay Kang, Adam Kaplan, Jack Sanchez, and Sara Ellberg. Philip Kim, thank you—again and again and always—thank you. All my love and appreciation to Matt and Estelle Konar Sr., and to my parents, Matt and Denise.

ONE

"I got it last time," I say.

But the ringing keeps on so I pick it up and a couple breaths cripple by on the other end, and on my end, or rather, what would be our end—because I'm staggered out on my grandparents' bed and my grandparents, they're in this too, they've got me, there in the middle, and we're all laid out because it's morning now, but still we haven't slept and the three of us, we're all dressed up, and what could be different about us, besides the fact that I'm eighteen and they're in their eighties, is they go to bed in their shoes, but I've given up on all that, all that outrunning at any given moment and while I'm on the phone there's this dumb flopping mutter that I shout through, because I know who it is and even if the caller has never been shown affection this is no excuse.

I hang up. The ringing starts again.

"Will one of you pick up the phone?" Dziadek asks. He can't do it. He has two on either side of him, but he won't answer. We're hemmed by telephones, by button, by wire—the

idea is to have ourselves surrounded from any point through-
out the house, we have modern, we have past, they beep in
pastels, sing in primary, they hook, they cradle—they're made
ready for our hands so we can be warned when we need to
leave.

My grandmother wonders who it could be. In her wondering she flexes, readies her body to fold or shrink, whatever the
avoidance of disaster might require.

"It could be anyone," Babcia says. "It could be anyone but
your sister or my sister or your brother or either of our parents.
They won't call."

"Because they're dead?" I ask.

"No one should assume anything," Babcia warns. "They
were all proud and none of them was buried properly."

"My mother's name was Esther," Dziadek says.

"That's my name too," Babcia points out.

"I know," he says. "Esther." And he reaches across me to
take her hand.

"That means you knew my name before you even knew it
was mine," she says.

"I know," he says. And then the mattress starts to leak
because the mattress is made of water and my grandfather's
boot heel has punctured its surface. He leans toward my grandmother. They make brief, contained noises of happiness as the
water leaves the mattress, their bodies sinking lower into the
bed. Then, suddenly, they part.

"It seems a good idea not to enjoy things anymore," Babcia
says.

They go back to admiring their cowboy boots, because actually, they're not wearing shoes. They're wearing cowboy boots,
they've always worn cowboy boots, it's their original footwear.
These are the first things they bought after leaving Poland.

"Will someone please pick up the phone?" I say. "I got it last."

And so Babcia calculates what's nearer, the touch tone behind her head or the rotary on the nightstand. She goes for the touch tone.

"Hello. Yes, yes, she is right here," she says, and the receiver mouths toward me so fast I have time only to think of how I don't know how to talk.

"I'm sorry?" I say.

And then she says my name so I know it's her, the one that's always getting scraped by a curtain. I've noticed that wherever she goes there are curtains. And small, stained tables. Bits of glass. Doors, sometimes chairs, bathtubs too, and her body slurs against it all so fast that I could forget the proportion of one thing to another if there weren't sudden peals of her voice to my mind, wherein I cover her mouth with my brain and her mouth disappears, taking my thoughts with it so that the white erase of her voice becomes my sole unit of measurement.

"What do you want?" I ask.

She cries a little. She says this is her one phone call. As in the one.

"So," I say. "That's for real? They really only give you one phone call?"

She goes on to explain that this might be more of a cliché than the truth because she's called a couple of other people before me but they weren't home, they were off—who knows what they were doing.

"So what am I?" I ask.

"Number three," she says.

"That's good. Number three. I must be pretty important."

"You are," she says, "you are important."

This is what she tells me. But I made some of it up.

"What do you need?"

She needs me to get her out of there. Inside there are a whole lot of men who would take advantage of a woman like her, and there are other women too, creatures with tongues worn out and necks amuck; it's all uphill as far as being human goes in there and she realizes she isn't much different and so this is frightening.

"Do I look okay?" she asks me.

"I wouldn't know. I haven't seen you for years."

Then she starts to cry again.

"You look good," I tell her. "You look good."

"Please, just get the money. Get the money so I can get out of here."

"I'll get the money."

"Thanks." And then there's this pause, then she says, "So how's school? You must be graduating soon."

"Not really."

"You'll be the first one to graduate from high school," she says. "The first one from my side at least."

But I think even she can tell that I'm not thinking about that.

"How'd you know I was here?" I ask. "How'd you know where to find me?"

"A mother always knows these things," she says. And then her time must have run out because she hangs up.

"What was that about?"

"That was my mother."

"A bad person," Babcia says. "Came from a bad family, came into our family, and now look."

"Can I have some money?"

"Of course," Dziadek says, and he hands me a five.

I catch a bus across town. I try to pay the dollar but the driver won't let me, she says, oh no honey you only have to pay two of those quarters since you're so young. I don't correct her because at this point, anything saved is good. I go to my little brother's school. I haven't been to school for three or so years now myself, but I know that I've probably changed more than school has, which means that I probably shouldn't hit back and I probably shouldn't make eye contact with anyone but my brother. Which is fine, because he's the only one I want to see anyway. My brother is a freshman and he always has about five dollars. I figure five dollars can't hurt in helping our mother. I find him in the cafeteria, sitting alone in the back. It takes some looking to recognize him because when I last saw him—this was two years ago—we hadn't eaten in a very long time, and now he's wide and drinking out of a straw.

"Hey," he says. "When'd you get out?"

"Yesterday."

"What do you want?"

I explain the situation. He's not impressed.

"We're family," I say.

"About that—"

"Yes?"

"It's come to my attention," he says, "that you and I probably do not have the same father."

"You sure?"

"Positive," he says. He wears paper napkins splayed across his lap. The polite napkins make him even less recognizable to me, even more of a stranger.

"Who are your sources?"

"Listen," he says, and he blows a bubble in his milk. "I'm Mexican. Hispanic. You know, a bean bandit? When I grow up I'm supposed to whistle at girls all day from the back of a pickup truck but my ancestors may have been kings."

"What are you trying to say?"

"Look at us. Just look at how different you are next to me."

"Of course we're not the same. I'm older, you're younger."

He bites into his sandwich.

"That good?"

He nods. He knows I like to act as if I want something just so I can turn it away. So he doesn't offer. He just wipes his hands with one of those napkins instead. I'm jealous of that napkin. But I try to focus on the problem at hand, instead of the one balled up in his fist.

"Are you liking the new place?" I ask.

"I'm pleased with the situation. My new fosters—they are a pleasure."

"They have good food there?"

"Definitely. We eat chickens. And cheeseburgers, you know, which are hamburgers with cheese on them? And once a week we have an ethnic meal—that means a meal outside the American culture—so I can learn more about my Mexican heritage."

He reaches over with his napkin. He tries to wipe my face. I didn't know I was so dirty. Somehow, being around family always makes me aware of it.

"It's a lot better than the stuff they've got over at your grandparents I bet."

"They're your grandparents too."

He wipes my face harder, which is something people do when they want to argue with you but choose to change the subject instead.

"So when did you get out? I heard that you were involuntary. Which means you didn't have a choice but it's not exactly against your will."

"I had a choice. Just not at first."

"So when? When did you get out?" He waves his fork at me.

"You know," I say. "I remember when we were little and my baby teeth weren't falling out but my adult teeth were coming in. So I had two sets of teeth. And you had none. I had a stutter, two coughs, and three ways of screaming. And you had none. I had too much. So I tried to give you what I could. I tried to take care of you—"

And then we're interrupted. This wheezy kid comes and sits down opposite us. His eyes are crossed. He looks like he got hit in the head with a lollipop. He probably did, but I don't think it was my fault. I wouldn't have wasted something so sweet on a kid like that.

"Hey Miguel," he says. And then the kid starts shoveling it down like the melee of skin he is, all crossed up and full of nothing. I think that plate of peas knew more than he did.

"Hey Christopher," my brother says. "You ready to run some miles after school today?"

"Let's do it."

"I'll motivate you," my brother says. "We'll motivate each other."

"Yeah," says Christopher. "They can't keep us off that team forever."

"Christopher," my brother says. "This is a friend of mine."

"I'm his sister."

"Really? You don't look related." Christopher tilts his brain towards me as if to empty it.

"She's my half-sister. Which means we share half our blood."

"Much of our blood comes from our mother," I add.

"That doesn't mean anything," my brother protests—slow and loud, as if he's talking to someone who can't hear, and I didn't know that Christopher had problems hearing our language, but his deafness shouldn't matter to me anyway, because this is between my brother and me, no one else—"I'm trying to tell you," my brother insists. "Our blood is not the same."

"I know," I say. "I have more of it than you." His stare follows me as I leave the cafeteria. The whites of his eyes make me want to forget we're family. I want to forget so I can have the chance to remember things over, differently maybe, or at least for keeps.

I remember when we were kids and our mother took us to get tests. This was when the disease first broke. They gave us pictures to color while we waited. My brother, he got lucky, he got one of those mazes like on a placemat in a pancake house, one of those things where the object is, quite often, to wend a line through ducts and tunnels of air-fat without stopping—bad as it is to stop it's worse to start again, and that hesitation mark in crayon could be larger than anything, larger than running headlong your overestimations of what constitutes an ending. He wasn't doing it right. He wasn't strong enough. And so I helped him out, we hunched together over the paper. We drove those lines hard and fainted. We fainted because the nurses had taken blood-loads from us for the test. The results were negative, but in that good way, as in negative, your kids don't have that disease, but bring them back later anyway, this is a new thing, we don't know much about it, we could be wrong.

When I finish remembering the day of the disease, I go to find my brother again, down by the tracks where it doesn't matter what side you come from just so long as your timing is right, and the finish line is near.

My brother is pushing his body around the track so I have to run to keep up with him. We run side by side. He pants. He wears tiny shorts, checks his watch to see what kind of time we're making here. The ground moves beneath us in a way I can't quite trust, but I figure I can work with it, this is good, this is how things get done.

"It's about our mother," I say.

"She's a bad person."

"Sure, but she always made sure we were clean. She'd never let one of us leave the car without our hair combed. And if there was a hole in our clothes she'd sew it up."

"She was good with a needle all right."

"It was always important to her that we looked like presentable," I say. "It was always important that we smelled decent and appeared normal and I don't know, maybe if you'd just think about that for awhile you'd see."

His pace quickens.

"Look," I say, "she didn't mean to let those things happen to us."

"But she knew. She knew they were happening, right?"

"Probably not. Maybe."

"She knew."

"That's true," I admit. "She did."

Then he stops and stoops down and takes from his shoe a five dollar bill damp with sweat. He always put things there for safekeeping, because it seemed like the thing to do. I know he's just helping me so I'll leave, but I take it anyway. And then what happens next, I don't know, I just—there's this girl running by us and she could be me because she's mean but she isn't me because she's in another body, one that's blurred in its advancing legs, one that's beaded in its cruel perspiration. From a face all swollen with her mouth she gives my brother news: he sucks. And so I'm running up beside her and realizing that no, she can't be me because to myself I'd only whisper. "You talk like a trap squeaking out," I tell her. "You've got knuckle significance," I say. So of course, she hits me first. She has all the grace of soap in a sock but her hands don't clean me, she just lays me down, she lays me all to splattery and my eyes, they're outbleared by some sting she's put there, thick as signature. And I choose only to lie there, because when you're the one who gets hit first you can lie about anything.

The principal sits me down in her office. I sit with a bag of ice and watch the water sneak onto her desk. She's the voice of reason if the voice of reason is a wanting to make things right, and she gives me the kind of smile that asks for my side of the story.

I want to tell her that, ethically, I'm looking for something in the way of loving-kindness. Somewhere, I want to tell her, somewhere I'm a virgin without loopholes, an inch of well-meaning nature, a tremble on the brink.

Instead, I apologize for my actions, which is really the same thing.

"It doesn't really matter who started it," she says. "I know you're new here, but the suspension's the same. You'll have to go home now. Take some time to think."

"I can always use some time to think," I admit.

She pats me on the hand.

"It's hard to be new isn't it?" she says.

The ice has leaked away. My eye isn't swollen anymore but now my nipples are sticking out, and so I fold as much of myself as I can. Over and into, where no one can see what should be leaving. I don't know how to talk to her. In talking to women who are strangers I lose half my weight, most of it in flesh, but some of it in bone too.

"I need to notify your guardian." She hands me the phone. "Please dial."

I'm thinking of my grandparents making the shapes of old people beneath their sheets and I just don't feel like interrupting their gazes bootward. So I dial another number instead, one that I'm not even sure is good anymore.

On the telephone, the principal says that I need to be picked up immediately because I'm somewhat injured and in need of familial comfort. She listens to the parental concerns on the other side and assuages them somewhat. She looks puzzled for a moment, but then she gives directions to the school and repeats them twice. Just so there can be no mistakes.

Some twenty minutes later, some thirty, double that, sixty minutes later, a man walks in. This is my father. He's as small as he ever was, but I don't notice how much I've grown now, standing at his shoulder. We both stare at his shoes. I don't know why he doesn't want to look at me but I figure it might have something to do with my face. He can probably tell that while people touched me I had to think of something else, and so I thought of him, and I didn't know what he was like so I made it all up, I thought of him going to the movies, I thought of him crying during the sad parts and his tears were always as I wanted them, they were fat and tremulous and quick at the downfall. They were piteous and salty and well-groomed. Mostly, they were for my mother.

His shoelaces are untied. I bend to tie them, even though I'm not so good at knots, but he just pulls me up from the floor and takes me out to the parking lot. We get in the car. He turns the key. This gives us some music. I think it is sixties music. I think it is from the eighties. He tries to start the engine. All the elementary kids are getting out of class now across the street. They walk past the car as it sputters. They walk to the park sucking anvil-shaped popsicles. And then the car, it starts, and we're riding down the street so fast.

"I ran a red light," he says to himself. This is also the first thing he says to me.

"How red was it?" I ask.

Apparently, my father is a nurse. He tends things. In white rooms. He packs things too, stuffs piles of cotton into whatever's empty. The war on emptiness, he informs me, will be fought with the pile.

He leads me on a tour of his apartment. It has piles all around it. He tells me proudly that he throws away nothing. The apartment has high ceilings and the air just kind of sulks over the piles and the tops of our heads with nothing to do but claim some affection for the space that has been left alone, that brief reprieve from an organized sadness.

"This is my kitchen," Dad says. "This is where I prepare the food that I eat. I eat twice a day, once in the morning before work, and again, in the evening, after work. Sometimes I might also eat in here. But usually, I eat in front of the television."

"This is my living room," he says. "The television is in here. I don't watch the television much. Except maybe when I eat."

"This is my bedroom," he says. "I sleep in my bedroom. I might sleep four, maybe five hours a night. I walk in my sleep.

Once, I walked right into the kitchen. When I got there, I prayed. I prayed that your mother would come back to me. Then I thought better of it. And I prayed that your mother would never love anyone as much as no one loves me. Then I made a sandwich."

"How do you know?"

"What's that?"

"How do you know? I mean, if you were sleepwalking, how do you know?"

He pulls on his beard, thoughtful.

"The kitchen counter," he says. "It had crumbs on it. And a knife was out."

I look past him, towards his patio, which is free of heaps. It overlooks the swimming pool in the courtyard. Many of the residents have taken to its chlorinated waters. Outside, it seems, there's nothing better to do than be weightless.

"So," Dad says, and he gestures to the patio. "Would you like to sit?"

We watch people sun themselves. There's a couple of kids in the pool, fighting over pennies at the drain, and a buoyant woman floating on the water, with the sun glaring around her so that the white of her bathing cap becomes a point of reference for whatever you feel like referring to—not just the fact that this pool has a shallow end and a deep end, but that this whole one-day-at-a-time thing is wrong, all wrong, and sometimes a pill is a good idea.

"Your grandparents—"

"They're okay."

"They didn't tell me you were out," he says. "I think you should know," he says, "that I didn't know."

"That's okay."

"How long were you in there, anyway?"

"Almost a year. I think. That's right. About a year. But only the first couple of months were involuntary. Then I just stayed."

"My parents—they paid for it? It was a nice place?"

"They paid for it. It was a nice place."

"Must've cost a lot. I bet you could've gone to a good college for that much."

"It was worth it," I say. "I never felt better," I say.

The buoyant woman goes underwater. I watch her hold her breath, float beneath the surface, begin to peel.

"Why'd you leave then?"

"Because," I tell him. "Because first I was seventeen, then seventeen and a half, and yesterday, all of a sudden, I was eighteen."

"I see," he says.

"And that's how I am now. Eighteen. Just like yesterday."

"I know," he says, and he looks as if he'd like to know that I'm real and I consider putting my hand on his to prove it, but I don't because I don't know how to touch living things, how to stop, where to go, especially when they're family, especially when they're people who have parts that could fit into mine, even though they aren't really supposed to I guess, and whether that's because they're people or because they're family I'm not sure I'll ever know.

I lace my hands together. He pulls his beard, even though his hands are laced too, just this tug, from one thumb to another.

"When you turn eighteen," I tell him, "that's it. You're an adult and it's off to the adult ward with you."

"Yes," he says. "That's a bad place." And his face organizes itself like faces do when people are busy knowing what is important to them. "Wait here," he says, and he gets out of his chair and walks, no, he actually marches, he marches urgently into the kitchen, and all the while he's calling back to me, he's telling me not to go anywhere, he's telling me not to move.

He comes back with a plastic bag that's stiff with ice. It smells like it's developing the germ for its own death.

"Thanks," I say, and I start to put it over my eye. But I can't feel my eyes and I can't even remember which one is hurting anymore, so I just shuffle the bag around until he takes it away from me.

"No," he laughs. "Open it."

Inside is an umbilical cord. I thread it around my knuckles, I finger the string of it, the blue and preserved code, it coils, it feeds, it wraps around my wrist twice, and I'm looking at it and even though I don't want to believe it's mine I know that it must be, because it makes sense now that a person has to start somewhere.

"I thought you might want it back someday," he says.

"Thanks."

"So what do you want to do now?"

"I have ten dollars," I say. "I'd like to go to a movie."

TWO

"In conclusion," he says. Everyone says the world is forked, it's put my brother out to posture, now he's a winner, some semi-stranger with shoulders high. They whisper it in the bleachers. They murmur it around the flagpole. I hear that he's making the best grades and managing the bus system like no other and he never hits classmates and his voice is cracking in all the right places. I watch him on the debate team where his hand argues against the angle and the clock. My brother's good.

After the meet, I corner him by the water fountain. He wears his new foster family well, I tell him. It's done him a lot of good, I can see that, and he's my half-brother, so in a way, that family is part mine too. I want to meet them.

"Sure," he says. But that statement doesn't move fast enough. While it makes its way into my reach, word-first, he still has time, he's able to consider the possibilities, and he adds, "Just get your diploma first."

So I take a test. The test wants to know if I'm generally

equivalent, brain-wise, to other teenagers fit for survival, based on the information given in the following excerpt.

My time runs out during the test. I fail, but I don't return to my brother empty-handed. I bring him a letter that says I will be eligible to take the test again in another month.

"Do you have a job at least?" he asks.

They're hiring down at the place where cars ask windows for chicken. I show them my letter there. They think enough of it to seat me by a button that puts my voice out into a world of front seats where everything is tendered. When I see my brother again, I bring him a pay stub, and some wings.

"Are those the only clothes you own?" he asks, and he points with fingers cased in shine, his teeth furring with bucket-meat.

Next paycheck, I go down to the store where all the clothes hang and I put on the clothes, the ones the saleslady claims are in my size. They seem too heavy to me but I don't know anything. I only see that this newness is my leg, my arm. I'm inside of it.

I wear the new clothes for my brother. He corrects my buttons, and then he looks at me and says, "I love you, you're my half-sister, we share the same mother, and I think we both might have her jaw, but you don't look right. You need to try harder."

My mind's made up. That's what I tell my father while he puts me to bed. He asks me if I'm sure that this is the right thing for me to do at this point in my life. Yes, I say. Because I figure that this is what trying harder must mean. My father wants me to have all the information before I make such a big decision. So he shows me a book about what it's like to spend a year in school. He points out the spirit squad, the prom system, the empty margins that stand as proof of his own lonesome teenage lunches. I close the book. Its cover is stamped with a carnivore, cross-town rival to my brother's endangered species. "I'll go here," I say.

"You'll be starting all over," he reminds me as he tucks me into bed. "Don't forget," he says, and he plugs in the nightlight. But I could argue with my father that forgetting is essential to the proper function of memory. I know this fact because I study at the public library all the time. I forget a lot there too though, because I'm so busy watching my brother.

He seems to prefer the illustrated versions of things, the saturated mock-ups of real life organizations such as the spleen and the vowel. So we have that in common, and this resemblance comforts me. But then I see him lick his finger to turn a page, and this looks like something he's learned from the woman who picks him up precisely at five. I've seen her bleacher-side in be-kittened sweatshirts, waving signs that rename my brother, tell him to go, he can't be beat, he's the best. When the librarian stamps my book and peels back the rubber, I see them exit and I know it's final. My brother belongs to other people now.

The first foster that was the beginning of parents for us was extensive and stole our food. She had fingers too fat for bending so we'd open jars for her all day, and when we got tired of opening jars we'd go hide under the bed and she'd haunch over and try to grasp us with an arm, but the arm would get caught and flop, glow white with threat, and my brother would set her free which was always a mistake because then she'd return with a broom and crouch there, poking. The second and third fosters were fragrant sisters who passed us back and forth because neither thought they could do us justice, they'd find our dents and mouth blisters and day-wrongs, and heave great sobs and herd us tighter to their fronts. The fourth I can't remember because I told myself not to. The fifth was a person I stole from regularly. The fifth had a kid of her own, a teenager who licked the heads of matches all day in practice for my moister points. I figured I was owed for this unwelcome wetness, so I stole even harder. The sixth foster I can't remember because I wasn't there, I was in the hospital, but I heard she was the same as the fourth, just with bigger closets. And this is the seventh. She's the first mother that belongs only to my brother. We are used to having different fathers, but a mother is something we've always shared. This seventh here, she's original.

At school I make friends. Three debate team girls with eyeglasses on high. They don't really talk to me except to say that certain seats are taken. In detention, I sell my prescriptions to the kids that don't achieve, the ones who roll joints for bookmarks and fall asleep in class if they know what's good for them. I donate these proceeds to the school spirit box. My school has dry lawn, asbestos worries, rhythm problems, mascot trouble. The unachieved kids ask me how I got so lucky. They want to know how to have shudders big enough to warrant pills. "In conclusion," I tell them, just in case the debate team girls can overhear. My voice maintains its failure. The marching band quavers by, boasting one pair of cymbals and three ideas of how to end that song.

A week into my education I find myself jumping for air. In gym class, we bounce, swag, settle, we're doing one two three and four and when I touch my toes I can see a distance with a ladder in it and a man on top of the ladder, thumbing a ceiling leak. He's too busy with the leak to notice that I see him, I remember him, the way he used to buy me candy and make me guess which hand. I guess he's a janitor now. He used to be important. Once, he was my mother's pimp. He was the second pimp, the last.

And he was better than the first, who was always sneezing into a hat. The second wasn't so bad. He used to hypnotize me every day. To make me eat my vegetables and honor and obey. He had to. I was always forgetting the please. I was always forgetting the toilet-flush, the closed mouth breathe. He'd sit me down and wave a watch. It was a skill, he said, that he'd learned as a prisoner of war.

He can't put that dozy finish on me anymore but he still lives and knowing that he lives has an effect on me. The effect is located on the inside of me, somewhere between the ulcer on my spine and the humors in my marrow, and it moves me to walk him home after school, to a set of four walls with the stuffing out. He says he stopped selling people because his liver gave out; first it got soaked and then it got rabies, but he's off the list now and fitted with donation. He's covered in bite marks from fleas and his ex-wife. She cradles a piglet that looks like a potato and does a new dance called the fluke, which mostly involves sticking out her tongue. In the bedroom, he covers her with a blanket so we can have a little privacy. On his dresser is a trilogy of walnut shells, a bottle of suntan lotion, and a change purse. I touch them all.

I ask him if he has anything of my mother's.

"Just the things I can't forget."

There are things I'd like to remember about my mother, and I tell him so.

"Like what?"

I tell him that it's only the happy times I want to think about.

"I could arrange that," he says.

His tone makes me think. As I think, I fiddle with the walnut shells. Nothing lurks beneath their musty husks, but I keep checking, just to be sure, until he smacks my hand away from his valuables.

"How much?" I ask.

He names his price. It's slippery and located somewhere on an incline. Which is to say, he wants my forgiveness.

"I can't do that anymore," I say. "But let me think."

When I'm not at school, or with the last pimp, I continue to spend my time in the library. In the library I can watch my brother over the top of my books. The books claim that my subconscious is the real brains of the operation, but my brother is smarter and people want him. I watch and try to learn. About how he makes them feel understood with a nod. About how he slides out of the way when he's in an aisle that's too narrow and reaches up when the shelves are too tall or a person's too short. He even carries books for ladies who have full hands. But he'll only look in my direction while reading to the blind.

After the bell rings, I find my mother's second pimp pawing through the grass on smoker's hill. He grunts, lifts things for inspection, tosses them over his khakied shoulder. When he spies the end of something good he inserts it into his mouth and motions me over for a light. We lean close together. His breath pouts.

"You should brush your teeth," I say. "Show some respect for yourself."

"I respect myself just fine," he says. "No thanks to you and your mother."

He mounts his lawn mower and idles there for a minute, because it's a good day out, and there's no one around to interrupt that roll of field, that change of cloud.

"Get back to work," I say. "And give me a straight line."

"Aren't you supposed to be in detention today?"

"You work for me now," I tell him. "I'll be the one asking the questions."

I want to ask the questions just so he'll talk over me. I'm only comfortable using my voice as long as I can't hear myself. That's why I try to get him to drown me out with his voice so I can practice speaking. I ask him to tell me how much she cared, I ask him to tell me how she didn't want to leave—all so I can whisper beneath him, because softer seems to make steadier what I say—and then I do to him what he used to do to me. I turn words into numbers so he'll fall asleep. I make him count backwards until he drifts off. And then I'm able to touch him without his knowledge.

When he wakes up we watch cheerleaders turn into a pyramid. On hand and knee those skirty girls set themselves up for a fall. We're watching them from beneath the old wooden bleachers. He fans himself with my latest history assignment. Which is a treatise about how I feel we as people should feel about the past. The girls tumble and he fans faster. My treatise flags and unfolds.

"It's good," he says. "But it needs work."

I've made him my new tutor because I could never understand what my old tutor was saying, she was always leaning over my shoulder, and speaking into my ear like it was a pocket and because I couldn't understand her she just became someone who taught the clock to slow. As a tutor, my mother's second pimp is easier for me to understand. We've grown up together, so to speak, and he's learned his lesson. I'm still working on mine.

"Can you be more specific about what I need to improve?"
I ask.

"That last part—you don't have me convinced. I'm not
sure of your convictions."

"You mean the part where I keep saying that it wasn't my
fault?"

"No. Later."

"You mean the part where I say I didn't do it and I know I
didn't do it but I feel as if I did it?"

"No," he says. "You should keep that. You're really onto
something there. It's the rest of it that's terrible."

And then I realize that he probably can't read, and I think I
express this not only by taking my homework away from him,
but by saying so as well. But I can't be sure because the cheerleaders are shouting the alphabet into a triumph so winning
that even my hearing is overcome by loss.

"Of course I can read," he says. "I've got a black belt in
karate."

He tugs the paper in my hand, takes half of it with him.
His pencil tears through to circle and scratch, he gnaws the
eraser, he pauses, he scrawls me a B-, then a B=, and then he
just gives up and draws an airplane.

"Did you go to a school too?"

"I went to a war. You know that."

"And then what did you do?"

"I met your mother."

"Was she like me?"

"No. More like her." He points to a girl embedded with the
final shape of someone who leads people to victory. She has
feral eyebrows and a birthmark that fronts like a spot of blood
at her throat, but still, she's prettier than perfect, and more
perfect than anyone I've ever seen.

"That girl has a locker right by me."

"In the springtime," he sighs, "she does track and field. In fall, it's aquatics. But they won't let her be yearbook editor again because people can't be yearbook editor twice. That wouldn't be fair."

"I can talk to her for you. I could see if she's interested."

"She's the captain. Captains are never interested."

"But she'd get a little out of it; you'd get a little out of it, isn't that how it works?"

"I'm through with that life," he says. "Don't you have algebra right now?"

"It already started."

"There's still time," he says. He tries to read his watch, but he has some difficulty with that, since I stole the watch the other day while he was taking a bath and the ex-wife was playing a game with the pig which involved pounding on its potato-chest with her fist and prying its jaws open so she could bury her sighs into its unbreathing throat.

The librarian is upset with me today. I've disappointed her by keeping my books late. She thinks I'm not doing so well. She won't let the books be with me anymore because other people need to learn too. I explain to the librarian that the books say that I can do anything if I want to hard enough. She just says that I owe her. So I take out more of them. I exceed my limits. When I exit, my brother's sitting at the curb. He's waiting for the latest mother to pick him up and I offer to sit with him awhile so we can solve questions together, important questions, like whether running away or getting lost are really just the same thing. That sort of thing. But he has his headphones on so he can't hear me, and judging by the side that I can see, his head bowed low so he's mostly neck, this might not be a bad idea.

The night before my big exam, the tutor lets me in. I didn't think it would be so easy to sneak around school, but there's no one around. It's just us and the alarm system resting easy in the dark. The blackboard's neat with findings, the microscopes hunch. Everywhere, fingerprints prone.

"Whatever happened to the other kid?" my tutor asks.

"What other kid?" I play with his keys. They make sounds like no one's looking.

"The boy. The little boy."

"He's his own person now," I say.

We don't need all the answers, just the ones for the exam tomorrow, which isn't open-book, isn't even open-note. My desk has bad views.

"Do you see him?"

"Sure I see him, I see him all the time, I'm going to see him debate next week."

"Was it permanent with him?"

"It turned out to be, I think."

"Does it show?"

"Only when you know where to look," I say.

"You know," he says. "You know I never meant to. Don't you?"

I'm sitting behind the big desk in the front of the room, and I don't bother answering him. He didn't raise his hand. In the big chair my feet don't touch the floor. I find the answer sheet in the teacher's desk. It shows me what's true, what's false.

"Is this how you learn?" asks my tutor, and he folds himself into a chair so that it has no choice but to accommodate him. I don't answer him. Instead, I just think about what I've really learned from my tutor. I think about how I used to trick my

brother's brain into thinking of other things whenever something wrong was done to us. I hypnotized him the speaking
way, not with anything that swayed or ticked. I'd say: You're
getting sleepy, very sleepy. You're sleepy because I say so, so
sleepy that you walk on the shore and see a million fish tremble
silver in the sand. You see fish flash like quarters, like dimes, you
see them glint like a summer's allowance, and spend themselves
into coins. Fish pretend to be coins because coins are too tough
to be bullied by anyone. And when you wake you won't remember anything except that sometimes, you need to be a coin too.
And when I snap my fingers now you've got to wake up. Wake
up now, brother. Wake up, because I say so.

The next day, at school, I figure out that if I don't stand
too close to the squad captain I can see past her to the inside,
down to the hinge. The captain's locker is busy with cameo
and rag, balls of hair torn from the brush, idols ripped from
subscription, the linty deletia of last semester's average furled
into corners. From its ledge, books pile and muster.

"Don't you hate it when they stick?" she says to me, and
her voice sounds younger indoors, the cheers she leads have
disguised her.

I don't want her to see what I have in there, but she's too
eager to help, she fists it in combination and that seems to
give her some sort of pleasure, helping me I mean, and then I
kick it and she likes that, so she kicks it too, and we're so con-
tent with this new itinerary that neither of us notice the tutor
standing behind us.

"Ladies," he says, but really, he looks at her. We step back,
he pries it wide. Now, anyone can observe my interior. I have
to stand in front of it so no one can see how there isn't much
to see, just vials and detention slips.

"If you ever have a problem again," my tutor says, "you know I'll always be here for you," and he rattles his keys at us and walks away with his eyes fixed on her uniformed body like she's a problem solved.

"That was strange," she says.

I'm trying to think of how to tell her that I knew him once, but that it was a long time ago. I was maybe eight, maybe nine. My mother didn't really have a choice back then, but someone did before her and someone did before that and so it went, and so I wonder—what am I supposed to do now?

"Usually," the captain says, "these lockers will open with a little pull."

I collect my books and stack them on the shelf, spines out, so she can see at least that I'm trying to get it straight. I take algebra, composition, history, geology, drawing for beginners. Next semester I'll take drivers education, and maybe I'll make a run for student council, or even choir.

"Do you know where I can get any drugs?" she asks.

Mostly, the hypnosis worked. His fixed-gaze methods, his commands in repetition. Bad habits he used to cure so easy; my brother wouldn't pee in his pants anymore and I wouldn't swear. But sometimes I'd pee my pants, sometimes I still do, and some of the time it's when I'm laughing but more often it's when I'm scared, like now, because I don't mean to hurt the captain, but I'm going to take her to him, I'm going to make a trade. This for that. A pretty captain for a happy memory. And if she doesn't want to cooperate, I figure that if I can just get her still I can use other methods, because I stole his watch the other day and it's ready at my wrist.

No persuasion is required to get the captain to come to my tutor's house that afternoon. Just the promise of some after-school needlework at a friendly discount.

"Only a little farther," I say.

She's skipped practice to be with me, she shares gum from her pocket and shows me how to do a cartwheel in the yard.

"In here," I say, and when I open the door the piglet runs out into the yard and bites a kid with a magnifying glass and then the piglet digs a hole, rolls in it, and jumps over a fence.

"Now look what you've done," says the ex-wife, and she goes weeping past us in a nightgown, her arms achieving a plea towards the neighborhood.

Inside, my tutor's sounding out words aloud. The words sound like a letter from an author who was angry and then died, someone who wanted to be with him, then died, some-one who didn't deserve that, but wanted it, who could do bet-ter, but wouldn't, and then she hoped it wouldn't work, that pill, and then she slept. He doesn't notice that we're there until the letter's all over and done and read.

"What do you need?" he asks, and he stuffs the letter un-der the cushion.

The captain just smiles and tugs at the bottom of her skirt with one hand, but she pokes me nervously with the other. She wants me to hurry up so we can go. People like her are used to thinking they can just leave whenever they want.

"I brought you something," I tell my tutor.

The captain's digging in her backpack, she brings up bills but I push them away and sit her down. I bring out his watch and wave it before her eyes. It's not so much that I want to control her. It's just that I want her to do as I say. I figure she's as good a trade as any for the happy memory I need.

My tutor snatches his watch away, and instructs the captain
to leave. He does it in the old tone of hypnosis, but there's no
use for those methods now because she's already shoved me
aside and run. The tutor takes me into the bathroom. My head
hits the tile floor because he's put it there and he's standing
over me again but he's not clapping his hands this time. He's
not making me count backwards. He's not even describing how
my body feels lighter than a feather that proves not all birds
eat fish.

"I want you to forget those days," he orders, but I won't
keep still so he hits me a little, not too hard but somewhere in
the mouth, just to make me behave and I spit a little red and
then he gives me that happy memory I've been asking for. He
gives it to me in exchange for staying still. He tells me that
once he had some friends over and they started making fun
of the way I talked but my mother stepped in and made them
stop, she said no one could treat her kid like that and then she
packed a bag, and then she unpacked it, and we sat on the curb
for awhile, we sat until she realized we weren't going anywhere,
and she carried me back inside, she held me at the doorstep,
and I choose to believe it all.

This is the end of debate. At the last meet of the year, my
brother does well in an argument for a better living. He adjusts
his tie, clears his throat. He's a smart show, avalanching about
something to fight for, and there are a lot of people out here
who like him for it, but only I know why he flinches when
he's slapped on the back. Or maybe she does too. She's sitting
there, the latest mother, I can see her worry for his posture like
no one has before, and when it's all over, I don't mind so much
when he goes to her, because it's quick, that kiss, and then
she goes to the car and he makes sure no one's watching and

there's a lot of people around but I know it's me he's speaking to because I'm the only one he looks at that way. With that raised eyebrow, that narrowed eye.

"I heard you got kicked out," he says.

"Just for a couple of weeks," I tell him, and if he knows I'm lying he doesn't want to prove it and if he knows there's no real cure for what we carry he tries to hide it by thinking that some things never happened, or at least, that they never happened to him, and then he yawns. He's still sleepy. He still sees fish pretending to be coins because bullies don't eat coins, and all he needs to do is sleep and walk and stay in school, and make something better of himself, just because I say so. Someday he'll probably even make something better of me. Just because I say.

THREE

Everywhere, orphans. Bastards too. Shelter-babies turned into lawn angels. I'm in front of my brother's latest foster home, spying. I rode my bike here to see his new family. From my view in the bushes I see thumb-suckers and scab-pickers and bed-wetters and more. They erect birdhouses, play tin-can telephone. They hide and they seek and they salt snails on the sidewalk. And over there, that's my brother. He's sitting on a fencepost, dipping into pomade to battle a cowlick. He folds the black wings of his hair back.

From the arch of a window a bell rings. A motherly voice too.

"Flossie, Olive, Cash, Duke, Jackie, Miguel, John-John, Smitty, Sara," the voice says. "Dinner!"

The children come out of hiding and put away their scabs and thumbs and salt. My brother wraps his comb in a handkerchief and joins them in the line at the door. I follow him closely and then too close. I give my presence away because I can't help but reach for him when he's near.

"What are you doing?" he demands.

I tell him they won't even know I'm here.

"That's not what I'm worried about," he says. "They never know who's here."

He warns me to behave myself by turning his back on me. I creep along behind him. Sometimes it helps. Not being looked over. Just overlooked.

We crowd ourselves into the kitchen, take up paper plates, and sidle by the repast: pancake salad and convertible bananas, corn capers and foibles of pork and envelope peas. We mingle with puddings over easy and puddings over hard, funny beans and peek-a-boo meats, potatoes baked crescendo. We help ourselves.

Around the dinner table, every mouth is occupied. It's hard to tell the family's faces apart in all that chewing, but I can still see my brother from behind a length of corn. The corn's kernels spell out some code on the cob. Something about how they know not what they do. My brother's guardians trot their dentures into the thighs of something flighty. The triplets moan into their pudding. A scarred blonde blesses her muffin. I hide my face with a crescent of watermelon, keeping anything that might identify me behind that seedy shield. The family tosses their bones onto a bone-plate at the table's center. While the bones rib each other I sit and watch my brother, happy enough, until this mustached eight-year-old tries to take what belongs to me.

First I see his fingers tapping by my plate, and then I see his eyes mapping the distance between my potato and his mouth. Now he seizes my potato, and bite by bite it leaves my world to join his stomach. I start to protest, but Mustache continues to help himself to my plate, tweaking his mouth-hairs in my direction all the while. I have no choice but to defend myself by stabbing him with my fork. Unfortunately, this gesture doesn't help me go unnoticed. Mustache squeals. My brother drops his corn and squints, the guardians put away their meat, the blonde sets aside her crumbs. The entire assembly of eaters goes quiet. And I can't help it, I'm so loved up by hate that I stick Mustache with my fork and demand that he cough up what's rightfully mine.

"What do you think you're doing?" my brother asks me, and he snatches the boy out of my reach. Tears collect in Mustache's lippy fur. For every tear he drops a murmur goes up from the family—they wonder aloud how one of their own could be so mean.

"Which one are you anyway?" the female guardian wants to know.

"Maybe it's that new one," the male guardian says. "You know, the one with the embryo snafu and the delinquency situation?" He lifts my chin for inspection.

"When'd we get a new one?" a skinny kid asks from under her overbite.

"That's my sister," confesses my brother. He confesses it quietly.

"Are you pregnant dear?" the female guardian coos. She inserts a finger into my belly button, tests the waistband of my skirt with a snap.

"That's my sister," my brother repeats. He confesses it loudly now.

They look at me. They look at him. They look at me. They look at me closer, with eyes wide, with mouths waiting to wallow in disbelief.

"I'm his sister," I admit.

Later, while I'm being punished in the garage because it's only fair, the female guardian tries to tell me that Mustache didn't know any better. I tell her that this kind of excuse only goes so far. Even I know that, even if I'm good for nothing and nothing is getting worse these days, even it's getting darker round the zeros and longer at the nil. The female guardian blinks at me. She says that's not what she's trying to say. What she's trying to say is that Mustache is blind and he grabs at everyone's plates because his eyes can't relate to his own dinner. I argue that Mustache should've had the decency to enlighten me about his blindness. "He can't speak," she says. "Or hear," she adds. And then she gives me my punishment. She wants me to write that I will be a better dinner guest and mind my manners and act my age and pass the butter when people ask—a hundred times.

I begin. I write that I will be a better dinner guest—but then I forget the other words. I try to remember them, but I can only remember the dinner part and the guest part. This is because being a guest is something I'm familiar with. I've been a guest in lots of places: closets, gurneys, mirrors, cautionary tales, that mud puddle at school, that patch of track before the train. I pick up my pencil, but I can't concentrate because my thoughts are in the way. My thoughts keep on about how I was a guest in the hotel where my mom almost died but had a baby instead.

Back then, I was four years old and when I laughed, I laughed with my mom. When I wasn't laughing my mom was trying to make money by bending over to pick strategically placed handkerchiefs off the street. Our room was a good room and we always tried to pay for it. We had a roof above us, and a leak. Under the leak my brother was born. He was a shapely little baby with a suntan and a pompadour. We were lucky that the leak fell into his mouth and fed him because my mother's breasts weren't squirting in those days. Even though I was young, I realized that a leak alone couldn't feed my brother. Something needed to be done, so I tried to fix my mother's breasts for her. I fastened my teeth on the lefty and pulled, but that particular breast withdrew, it frowned, went blue, threatened to sour.

That left breast got sore at me. I believed that my chances with the right might be better, since it was centered and friendly, and at the beginning that chipper sack cooed in my hand, but when I tried to nurse it back to health it began to chortle. It laughed at me for being so childish. So I tried to be adult about it, I struck the breast and bossed it, choked it till it wept a sulky drop. My mother woke up squealing. My brother squealed too. I hushed them both.

I told them they had to be quiet, because if the hotel people thought we were too loud, they'd probably lock us all up in the linen closet where there weren't any leaks for dinner and we'd have to trap moths for food and bait the traps with light bulbs and pretty soon we'd be out of light bulbs because who carries light bulbs around anyway? That shut them up.

My mother took her cagey bust under the covers while I lay down on the bed next to my brother and made sure he caught every last drip of water that dropped near. Sometimes he'd get distracted—he'd drowse, babble, laugh, miss a bead—and I'd have to remind him that he needed to pay attention. He needed to catch those leaks and keep healthy and look out for himself. He offered me a drop. I took it. But in return, I gave him some advice. I warned him that if things turned out for him like they had for me, he had to remember something. He had to remember this. He had to be able to say, later, when he grew up and people told him that he was trash, that he was born once.

Back in the kitchen, I show the guardians the paper with my punishment on it. They're quiet as they read. The only sounds I hear are the happy noises of foster kids chewing and digesting, their bodies lumping with feed.

The female squints and frowns at the paper.

"It seems like you're sorry about something," she says.

"I am," I tell her.

"The slant of the 't' indicates regret," the male guardian points out.

"Would you like to rejoin us for dessert?" she asks. "Would you like to try again?"

My stomach growls at her in reply. I think the growl means that my stomach is above all this, but the female guardian doesn't pay it any mind, she just hands the paper back to me and gets pudding all over my punishment. She gets pudding over the parts where I was most sorry.

"What do you think Miguel? Do you think she's ready?"

To the guardians my brother says something about second chances. He says something similar to me but I think there must be a last chance in it too, somewhere.

At the table, I sit back down by Mustache.

"Mustache," I say. "I'm sorry."

But the hairy boy doesn't even turn in my direction. It occurs to me that showing him my regret might be better, so I push my most contrite and athletic drumstick in his direction. He still fails to accept my apology, and this is when I realize that nothing I could do would ever be enough. I could bite my tongue for him. I could light candles, scatter seed, bring him the head of foam from some dark beer. Walk on hot clocks. Wear mosquitoes in my hair. I could shed three drops of blood from my eyes. Hail a taxi. Wave palm fronds. And Mustache would just sit there in his barbeque stains. He would not be moved.

Then my brother steps in and shows me how to communicate. He takes my hand and strokes it with his fingers, from wrist to finger, penitent little touches of apology.

"I forgive you," I say.

My brother shakes his head. He points to Mustache, indicating that this procedure needs to be repeated for his benefit, so I take up the boy's hand. My fingers tap in tribute to the things that I'd take back if I could, and I throw in an extra touch for the things I may do to him in the future. In reply, Mustache nods and beams. His pinky plays tag in my palm.

"What does that mean?"

"He accepts your apology," my brother says.

"Well then," I say. "Well, thank you." And I take up my fork once more. I stab beans with it, and the beans wheedle down my throat. But I'm not hungry anymore. I've lost my appetite. Or maybe someone took it. I look over at Mustache. He seems to be good at taking things that belong to me. He's busy hustling down a bowl of honey jeebies with milk. He sucks down the prize that came with the cereal too. I had had my eye on that prize. It was a little compass. It only came in the most privileged boxes of honey jeebies, which numbered one out of every hundred, and I had been searching for that compass for months. I bet it tasted like the last one. Mustache smiles at me. I can tell that he sees how much this upsets me.

Mustache sees. I bet he can hear too. I bet he can speak and sing and shout and hold his own. I shout to everyone about his fraudulence, shout it over his eyelids while I'm peeling them back. But he thrashes silently in my grasp. I have to make him prove his potential volume. I twist his arm to make him shriek.

But he's too good at faking, the way every foster kid becomes good at faking after years of moving from family to family. Mustache just slops his mouth open and gapes, until the female guardian pulls me off of him.

"Who do you think you are?" she demands.

"Not him," I say.

The female guardian says I have to finish my dinner alone. She leads me down to the garage, seats me at the ping-pong table atop an old crate. She says she'll be more specific this time about my punishment and then she gives me a piece of paper.

I have to write a hundred times that I will never injure persons who are weaker than me. So I write that I will never injure persons who are weaker than me, and then I write that I will never strike persons who are weaker, poorer, stupider, stinking, pregnant, for real, or drunk. I write that twenty times or so. And then I write that I will never strike persons who are weaker, poorer, something, something, drunk—so long as they leave me alone and don't take my food. I need to keep my strength up because someday I want to go back and get revenge on the hotel people who locked us out after three days when we couldn't pay them. We tried to pay them in work, my mother and I. We said we'd scrub those floors pure, paint those stairs spotless. We were ready for whatever kneeling was needed but the hotel people wouldn't listen. They just pointed us down to the alley and kept our things: brother's blanket, Mom's coat, my book. My book had lions in it that popped up when I turned the page. I just know those hotel people tore my lions out. I know they threw the whole pride on the floor and stamped on them.

And I know even more: the hotel people fed the coat and the blanket to the closet moths and the moths went flapping over the city to make sure we didn't clutter it up anymore. They had tasted us, because in the weave of the blanket we had left a ripe and popular flavor. Moths like the taste of poor people, and they tried to get at my mother's breasts, but I fought them off. I struck them down, pummeled their wings, felt up their feelers. I made those insects beg.

Still, new coteries of moths thrashed down on us on behalf of the hotel people, they were trying to collect, they figured that if they couldn't rid the world of us they could at least get the money for the room. But we were too clever for them. We put on disguises as a family. We couldn't buy masks, so we did other things to disguise ourselves instead. My brother made his bones stand out and assumed a jaundiced shade. My mother's hair fell away. Then some of her teeth fell out too. A policeman helped her nose go nice and crooked. I wore sores. We disguised ourselves as weaker than we were.

When I finish with my punishment I sit back and try to gnaw on a bean or two but they won't go down anymore. They want no part in me. They take on a chill, and grow distant when I throw them against the door. I don't expect much help from them with that attitude, but the beans knock at the door till it opens and in the doorway is my brother, his stomach jutting out against his shirt at secretive angles. He's hiding something. But not from me. For me he lifts his hem to reveal a pie, cherry-perfect and laced at the pie-top. He brought two forks too.

"I didn't want you to eat alone," he explains.

FOUR

Together we look down on the origin of a snore, forty winks nodding lightly on a pillow, my father's face keeping time in a growing dark.

"I told you I had a dad," I say. "Now let's go."

But my brother won't move away from the five o'clock shadows.

"I bet you think you're better than me now," he says.

"I could never be better than you. I don't have what it takes."

"This is true," he admits, and he pokes the paternal shut-eye on the pillow. "It's just that you're so lucky," he says.

"I know."

"I mean, I don't even know where mine is."

"I know."

"What does he do?" my brother asks.

"Sleeps up a whole lot of bad nightmares."

"I can see that. The twitches give it away. What else?"

"Works. Prays. Writes letters to Mom."

"What descent?"

"Upwards. From people he's made into strangers."

"What are his pleasures?"

"Responsible gun ownership. Knowing best. This show on television about a lake of fire. Voting public officials into office."

"Any friends?"

"The mailman comes over a lot. And then there's me."

"Did he love our mother?"

"Does. Yes."

"Can you wake him up now?"

"I shouldn't."

"I just want to see what dads are like."

"He needs his rest."

"You're just saying that. You don't want us to meet."

"That's not true."

"You don't want him to have any friends but you."

He's kind of right, my brother, but also wrong. Really, he's the person that I don't want to have any friends besides me. But I don't say anything about that.

"My father can have all the friends he wants," I say. "Why should I care?"

"Good. Because I think I need a role model."

"You already have two role models. Your fosters. Three if you count me."

"I'm not counting you," my brother says, and he says it so loud that my father wakes up, he stirs from his pillow with a look of recognition for the kid at the end of his bed.

"This is her son isn't it?" he asks, but he doesn't wait for a reply, he just sits up and rubs his eyes and initiates a handshake. I watch him take in my brother's resemblance to our mother— her even eyes, her polite nose, all the enviables I failed to inherit—and as he recognizes these things his handshake grows tighter. And so begins another friendship. Just two people in love with the same woman brothering it out.

Instead of going out with me as planned, my brother builds conversations with Dad. Mostly, they talk about that stain I spilled onto the couch cushion just a couple of minutes ago. That plague-shaped stain might look unwanted, but it provides a great learning opportunity for my brother and Dad, because getting rid of the unwanted is one of their common interests. They make the process sound a lot more beautiful than it really is.

"Rub along the nap with that sir," my brother says. "Things usually come out easier if you don't go against them."

"I like the way you think," Dad says. This is the first time I've heard him say that to anyone who was not a thermometer.

"Sir—as a nurse—what's your take on bloodstains?"

"The first rule is to act quickly," Dad says.

"Makes sense."

"The second is never to mix removal products. If you do that you risk toxic situations. Remember that, Miguel. I don't ever want to see you in my emergency room just because you didn't respect the privacy of solvents."

"Yes sir. No sir, never. I won't. I swear."

"The third rule is to attack from behind. Your goal is to startle the ruin. Apply your treatment to the back of the stain and lift. This prevents the mark from traveling to the other side and spoiling everything."

"No one wants that."

"And have patience. Purification takes time. Repeat treatments may be required. Most of the time, they are. You have to keep working on it. You can't give up."

"I won't," my brother vows.

"And sometimes you have to give up. Some damage can never be removed, and you can ruin damage even more if you mess with it. In these situations, you just have to recognize there are other projects you can take on. And that the knowledge you've gained in this experience will give you a fighting chance against all those other stains. You just have to accept the damage."

This is where I come in. I put my head out the door and explain to them that this conversation they're having is interrupting the sleep I'm not having.

They apologize.

"I didn't know we were talking so loud," Dad says.

"It's getting late," I point out.

"Miguel called his fosters already," Dad says. "He'll be spending the night tonight."

I start to tell him that my brother's name isn't Miguel, that it's—

"I'm sorry," Dad says, confused. "I didn't realize—"

"It is too my name. I gave it to myself," my brother protests.

"Fine," I say. "I'll call you Miguel. Good night, Miguel."

My brother looks pleased that I've finally accepted this new identity of his. I don't know if he cares or not that this acceptance is dependent upon the fact that I'm about to replace him, because I don't stick around long enough to find out. I can do better than this, I figure. After all, what's the point in keeping a brother that I have to share with my father?

Down in the alley, I decide that I'll trap a new brother by sunup. I have my red dice and my best wishbone for bait. No one can resist those dice, they're always rolling high and getting even, and the wishbone has some clingy meat on it still. I figure I can catch a pretty decent brother with bait like this, or at least a brother that'll go to the movies with me once in a while. I circle the dice on the pavement with my rope and wait. Soon, the trap is approached by a gang of cats, a homeless pack of limpers with damp paws. At my ankles they are an abandoned legion, and they claim that they would make the best brothers for me. I can see their point. Despite our miniature needs and aptitude for affection, none of us are seen as very necessary creatures. So we have that in common. That and the mange.

When I don't respond favorably to the cats' offers of brotherhood, they circle the trap and mew. They begin to multiply themselves in vengeance. The grey one, that handsome one there, he mounts the girl in the tuxedo. They croon together, show me their overbites, make me watch. They make a nice couple, but their intimacy embarrasses me. They say they'll stop if I hand over the bait. No bone, no dice, I say. So other cats join them. The marmalade feral starts up with the patchy stray, the manx sire with the calico sweetheart, and so on and so fast, until it's all spots on stripes and fur aflight. The cats promise to stop if I'll just throw them my bone.

The sound of their howling unions makes my eye tear, but before I have a chance to surrender, a different kind of paw ventures out into the trap and pockets the bone. It's a human paw. I can't see who the human paw belongs to, because its owner is shrouded in knits and newspaper, but I can see it roll the dice between frostbitten fingers. The cats scatter with all of the odds in tow; they lick the six of the dice and carry the two. On my end, I pull the rope tight around the human paw and follow it back to its beginnings, deep into a fray of mothy castoffs, a protective layer of trash wrapped tight where a person breathes.

What I have here is a small bundle. It could be anything from a swollen kid to a shrunken adult. In any case, it isn't difficult to shuffle this heap into the apartment, and past my father and brother since they're busy making vitamins together. They measure out lines of powders and whistle. I prop my catch up in the bathtub and remove the discard: grocery bags and sleeping bags and swaths of tape, coat after sweater after bandage. At the center of this waste is the old woman who'll be my demi-brother. She's not much to work with, just a cripple of a specimen with an entourage of sores, but I'll fix her. I'll make her new a person again. First, she just needs to let go of that cane because it's in my way, and it's blocking my view of what she could be. I manage to distract her with my razor and snatch the cane away while her eyes are averted to the blade. We hear a knock on the door. The old woman startles, she starts to weep. I clap my hand over her mouth.

"Who is it?"

"What are you doing in there?" asks the person I now consider my ex-brother.

"Working on my hygiene."

"For over an hour?"

"My teeth are trying to be whiter."

"Oh," he says, and he sounds pleased.

"Do you need to use the bathroom?"

"Oh no, no, take your time," the ex-brother says. "It's not a problem. I'll just, we'll just go down the street and find a bathroom. We were talking about doing that anyway, you know, going out. Maybe for a sandwich or something. You want anything? Can we bring you anything?"

I whisper to the old woman. I ask her if there's anything she wants, anything at all, and she gives me her answer, which is that she'd like people to know how it might feel to be a woman who once had a job but lost it, who had a house but misplaced it, who had an explanation for her illness but couldn't remember it, and so she had to come up with new reasons why her mind was wrong but the reasons were wrong themselves and the reasons made her worse with them, they upped the ante on what it meant to be a person and by that definition she wasn't a person anymore, she was—

I can't understand what the old woman's trying to get at, so I do the only reasonable thing you can do in a situation like this, which is to act like you never heard anything at all.

"Forget it," I say to my ex-brother through the keyhole.

While they're gone we go through all the belongings I have of the ex-brother's. Things I stole because maybe I saw this coming. Or things I stole because I thought that maybe if I stole them, it never would come to this. I'm not proud of myself. It's a good thing that my plan is light on the pride and heavy on pretend.

The demi-brother runs her hands over the items: comb, bus pass, flashcard, a length of floss, a fingernail clipping.

"Do you have any questions?"

"What does he do?" she wants to know.

"Debate, track, clarinet, ulcers. Goes to school. Comes home from school. Writes fan mail to his senator."

"Any friends?"

"His pastor. And then there's me."

"What foods?"

"Anything square."

"What descent?"

"Same as me, minus my dad, plus some other dad. We're not really sure who, but there are two possibilities. Once, my mother pointed to guy at a gas station. She said he was the one. Or maybe she was pointing to the parrot on the guy's shoulder. I'm not sure. And later, there was another man, or more specifically, there was a dead man in a funeral parlor. But I think she just said that so we wouldn't feel bad about slipping the ring off the dead finger."

"What are his pleasures?"

"Being better than me. Setting his alarm clock. Hearing me tell the story about the time we slipped the ring off the dead finger."

"I don't know if I really care for that story, " says the demi-brother.

"It doesn't matter if you like it. My ex-brother likes that story. So you like it too. Make sense?"

"I guess—"

"Good. Let's move on then."

But the demi-brother has other plans for our conversation, she settles back in a chair and crosses arthritic legs in preparation for a long prattle.

"I can tell you a story," she says. "Two babies were born to me. They battled in their crib and died once a day, every day. Their resurrections were swaddled and lively. Eventually, one smothered the other to death for good. I touched the dead baby. He was really dead. The other was really alive."

Her face is a sudden wither of loneliness that moves me to take the thin skin of her hand in mine.

"You don't have to think about those things anymore," I tell her. "From now on, you just have to think the things that I tell you to think about."

"What I'm trying to say is that I could be a really good mother to you because I've got more experience being a mother than a brother."

"I didn't bring you here to be my mother."

"But I could do your hair in the mornings and pack your lunch before school," she offers, and she strokes my ponytail.

"You really think you can be my mother?"

She nods her head. So I tell her exactly what such a role would require.

"My mother walked her injuries around in high heels eating cookies and leaving crumbs for us to follow her through town. We followed crumbs past the gas station, the post office, the hair salon. We followed those crumbs over into this old hotel so we could find her sprawled out in the lobby elevator with sticky buttons beaming red and white all over our mother's face. We got into the elevator and the elevator got stuck, so we were all stuck together in a box full of crumbs, and when they came to rescue us, the authorities, they took us away from her. They hauled us off and left our mother pressing buttons in the elevator. She pressed a six, she pressed a three, but really, she didn't go anywhere. That's what my mother did. You think you can be like her?"

The demi-brother frowns. She goes still, and then starts to gnaw at her knuckles. I take her vulnerability as an opportunity to put her in the hall closet. My father and the ex-brother will be coming home soon, so I have to hide her there. I prop her up between the softest coats and try to think of a good bedtime story. I've never been too good at bedtime stories, but the demi-brother is so sad that I want to try, just for her sake.

"Tell me about when I met my dead father," she suggests.

"I thought you didn't like that one."

But the demi-brother insists, her pale eyes pleading out from violet folds of skin.

"Just the last part," she says. "Just the part about how before I met my dead father, right before we took the ring, our mother told me that things were going to get better. She sighed and adjusted her pantyhose and patted me on the head."

"She patted me on the head too," I say, even though I didn't know it till now.

In the morning I go to the closet and knock.

"Are you decent?" I ask the demi-brother.

It's the kind of question I should know better than to ask. She sniffles in response.

"I mean your clothes. Have you got them on?"

The doorknob turns and the aged woman I've made in my ex-brother's image steps out.

"The pants are big," she complains. "The shoes are tight. The shirt's scratchy."

I pay no attention to her complaints, and slip an old report card into her front pocket. Just to make things more authentic.

"What's this?" she asks, fingering a lofty average.

"You never go anywhere without that, understand? It means the world to you. You know why?"

"Because you gave it to me?" she says.

This sounds good to me. To be honest, my ex-brother carried that report card around all the time because it told him that he was worth something, but this explanation seems superior.

"You're catching on," I say, and I hold my demi-brother tight, I squeeze her till she starts to cough. I'm starting to think that this demi-brother is even better than the real thing, if only because she'll always believe that prized possessions come from me. She coughs some more and covers her mouth, but fails to crook her pinky while coughing in the manner typical of the ex-brother. I let it pass. It wouldn't be fair, I realize, to expect perfection at this point.

"Are you feeling sick?" I ask.

"I have this problem—"

"Is it your ulcers again? Puny little fire-starters playing bully with your guts?"

"I've never—"

"We should put something in that stomach of yours."

The demi-brother brightens at the mention of food. She takes a few steps forward and that's when I notice our problem. It's wooden and crooked and scratched all over.

"Lose the cane," I say.

"But I can't walk without it."

I tell her that *can't* is a word we can't afford to use around here. I pull the cane away from her. It takes some pulling. She falls on her trundled behind.

"All that falling must have made you hungry."

She nods and sniffles.

I go into the kitchen and get a cookie and a napkin. I put the napkin around the demi-brother's neck and the cookie in her face.

"You ever had a cookie like this?"

"Only after someone else had it first," she admits.

I feed her a piece from my fingers. Her tongue kneels for it.

"More," she says, and she tugs at my pant leg. She looks up to me, but only in the way that the ex-brother did when he was small, from the ground and pleading. I figure that if she can pull off that trick, she can walk like him too. I portion the cookie out across the carpet so there's cookie, carpet, cookie, carpet, more carpet, less cookie.

"Go and get it," I say.

And so she limps from mouthful to mouthful, to fraction to piece to crumb, and if I squint a little this way and regard her in profile I don't see an old woman at all. I see only the advancement of someone who will learn to love me. When she reaches the final crumb she starts to cry.

"There, there," I say, and I pat her on the top of her head, right where the part is, a separation between hair and scalp, a strip of flesh so anonymous it could belong to anyone.

Once a week, every week, the ex-brother and I used to go to the old hotel where the desk bell is broken and so much more. It's the one with the elevator and the crumbs in it. Now I take the demi-brother there. She leans on my arm, casts filial smiles over the decay.

We try to feed the fish in the lobby together. The demi-brother isn't good at feeding the lobby fish. My ex-brother never would've flung feed so recklessly. He would've measured them out in his palm, dropped them spare into gold mouths. The demi-brother just confettis her reflection with the flakes.

"You'll kill them by giving so much," I tell her.

She protests that such a thing isn't possible, throws another heap on the surface, and starts to shake.

"Let's do something else," I suggest.

So we try to have a drink in the lounge area where the waiters watch two fleas race across a finish line of white powder. It's a tie. Just like old times.

"Whiskey please," requests the demi-brother.

"She'll have a ginger ale," I say.

When her drink arrives she's too weary to swallow. It leaks from the side of her mouth and wets her shirtfront.

"I have another idea," I say.

So we try to help out the old bellhop, the way we always do. He's a knock-kneed geriatric in dusty pants, forever dragging luggage up the stairs because the elevator is so unreliable. My ex-brother would've grabbed that suitcase away from him and taken the stairs by twos and threes, while the bellhop and I lagged behind. But it doesn't even occur to the demi-brother to help out when she meets the bellhop. She just bats her lashes and fondles his saggy bicep. Which is something I don't think my ex-brother would ever do, but I give the demi-brother the benefit of the doubt and carry on. I haul the suitcase up while the two of them follow me close behind, hand in hand.

"How long will you be staying with us?" I hear the bellhop coo.

"It's up to my daughter," she laughs. And this is where I drop the suitcase and extract my demi-brother from the arms of the bellhop. She stumbles on the stair. I tell her there's one last thing we need to do. I tell her that after that, she can do whatever she wants, be whoever she wants. I just need this one last thing, I tell her, and I push her up the stairs, onto the second floor, into the peeling hallway, in front of the old elevator.

"Press that button," I tell her. The demi-brother cooperates. She pushes the button to a white gleam and the elevator parts its doors with a squeak. We take our usual places, near the back, against the plush wall with the gum on it. The panel of buttons mocks us in their countdown; they pulse red, grow pale, shed light on our situation.

"What do we do now?" the demi-brother asks.

I inform her that this is the part where, as brother and sister, we discuss certain memories we have which may or may not have happened, so that if they didn't happen we don't have to think about them anymore, and if they did happen, we don't have to think about them anymore either.

"I'll go first," she volunteers, pushing all the buttons.

"Good," I say, because things are starting to look up for me, they're starting to come together. This is how it needs to be, just me and my demi-brother, remembering the old days

"Once," she says, "you and I were in a line waiting for soup and people kept cutting in front of us and by the time we got to the front of the line the soup was gone."

I assure the demi-brother that this did, in fact, happen.

"Now you go," she urges.

"Once," I say, "you and I were spanking each other because we had nothing else fun to do and every time I struck you—"

But I don't finish because the demi-brother isn't listening, she's too busy falling down as we go on the up and up, past the third floor, the fourth, the fifth, the sixth. As we speed we hear honeymooners rut in chorus while runaways count their cash; we hear ghosts bruise and quitters cough up in sinks. The demi-brother slumps in the corner. I'm afraid we're stuck like this, all of us people, that we'll never really arrive at the end. Amid the carpet stains her face stares up at me, its eyes crossing and uncrossing. Then, suddenly, at the seventh floor, we stop. A tall boy joins us and bends over the demi-brother. I'd like to act like I don't know him. But the fact is that it's hard to treat him as a stranger. I know him like the back of my hand, the front of it too, and all the impressions it's made on him over the years, those marks I spread so quick over my best of kin.

"What are you doing here?" I ask the ex-brother.

"We always come here on Tuesdays," he says. "That's just what we do," he shrugs. "Who's your friend?"

"She's the new you. You weren't being you. So I got a new brother."

She tries to shake his hand by way of introduction, just the way I taught her; she puts the thumb-bumping in there, she throws in the pointer straddle, the pinky mayhem.

"You can't do that," the ex-brother says, and then he turns to me. "She can't do that," he protests.

"Why not?"

"Because that's our handshake. We worked hard to come up with that, you and I."

"But you don't use it anymore," I argue, and the demi-brother nods in solidarity.

"That's just because it sticks out too much," he says. "I don't like to stick out too much. It makes people talk."

The demi-brother considers this. She brushes the hair out of his eyes and buttons his collar.

"Do they talk to you in your head and you talk back to them?" she queries.

He doesn't bother to answer her, he just pushes the button for the first floor so we can all hit bottom together. She brings her weary mouth to his ear.

"Because there's nothing wrong with you," she whispers. "There's nothing wrong with any of us, nothing at all, never was, don't let them tell you different," she says, and then she opens and closes her mouth a few times, as if there's something more to say, but if there is she never says it because she's too busy moaning through chapped lips.

"What do you think?" I ask. Because my ex-brother is staring at the moaning with interest.

"I think she's actually more like Mom," he says as he bends to her side. Then he takes the head and I take the feet. We hoist her body up and carry it out of the elevator. This comes easy to us. We're talented at it. I didn't think we'd know how to do it anymore, after all these years, after all these demi-people, fosters and nurses and family and all. But it turns out that carrying a sick body to safety is a skill you never forget after learning it once, like riding a bicycle in your sleep or begging for forgiveness.

After carrying her on the bus and through the street, up the stairs and to the apartment, we can't agree on where to deposit the demi-brother. The ex-brother wants to put her on the couch, but I'm leaning towards the closet. She wakes up while we're talking, she wriggles free and falls on the floor.

"That can't be good for her," the ex-brother says.

I prop her eyelids up, watch her pupils squirm.

"Are you all right?" I wonder.

"What's that?" she asks. "What happened?"

"You fell down."

"Fell where who?"

"She's disoriented," decides the ex-brother. "Let's get her onto the couch."

But when I try to help he pushes me away. He props her up with a cushion, and then all is revealed as the old report card falls from her pocket.

"Where did you get this?" he asks.

"I just wanted to keep it for awhile," she says through the filmy substance leaking from her mouth. "So I could be close to you. I haven't seen you in so many years. I haven't seen you since—"

The ex-brother turns to me.

"I think you'd better call your dad. She's really sick. And mixed-up too."

"You call," I say. "I have to stay. She's like a mother to me now."

And then my brother—I'm calling him that now because I'm realizing now that the jig is up, I can't pretend any longer that he isn't mine, there is no ex, no demi, only him—he mutters something under his breath and then he goes into the kitchen and begins to dial. He presses so hard that I can hear the buttons on the phone light up.

"Why did you kids leave me?" the old woman asks.

I remind her that she left us. Sort of. In another version of her life, not the one I created, but the one that came by accident.

"I don't think you have your facts straight," she slurs.

"Let's just say it was an accident," I tell her. "Let's just say the elevator got stuck."

My brother leans out of the kitchen, phone in hand.

"What's your father's name?"

"You mean you don't know?"

"I call him sir. I call everyone sir."

"Moses," I say, and I watch him wince but then he just gets back on the phone and asks for Dad by name, he says that it's urgent, and then he joins us on the couch. He takes up her hand and strokes it, but all the while he's looking at me like there's another question I need to answer.

"I didn't think it would mean anything to you," I explain. "Since Dad's not your real family—"

But the old woman interrupts.

"Of course it means nothing now that we're all together," she says. "I looked for you, and sometimes I found you, but you'd say you weren't really there, you'd say I was just making it all up. I'm not making it all up now again am I?"

"No Mom," my brother says.

I decide that it might be best to find out a little bit about this person while we wait. Maybe remembering who she really is will take her mind off of being sick for a little while.

"What do you do"? I ask her.

"Stay out of the rain and feed cats. Mostly, I read to cats. I read the newspaper, the street signs, the soda cans."

"And from whom did you descend?"

"Same as anyone else, minus their parents, minus their grandparents, minus their great-grandparents."

"What are your pleasures?"

"Keeping warm," she says, and then she stops saying anything at all.

We've done this before too, we haven't forgotten how to press an ear to a chest or check for the reflection of a breath or search a wrist for stirrings, and we do these things for a long time, over and over, ear to chest, finger to pulse, mirror before the nostrils, we look and find nothing, no stir, no beat, and then just to be sure, I try to give back her cane, but she won't take it, and that's how we know what's happened, because she never refuses anything.

What comes next we're not so used to. We never had to deal with this part before, the part where a woman closes her eyes and fails to open them again, but I figure that what concerns us now is preserving her body. So we take turns holding her jaw shut. My brother holds the jaw first. He's shy but he knows that if he isn't firm enough with that opening now, people'll have to lay her out and snap it, they'll break it if they bother with her face, they'll break it if they care for closure, and we can't have her buried that way, we can't have her lie beneath without being together. Then I take hold of the jaw. A minute passes, and another, and then a key turns, and my father walks in, he looks at me for an explanation, and with my free hand I point to my brother, because it's too late for a lot of things, but I know that she would've wanted it this way. She'd want everyone to know who we really are.

"This is Moses-Miguel," I say. "He tried to save her too."

FIVE

We see a bottle dance in the gutter. When the cars drive by, it tangos. When the wind blows, it twists. I've never seen a bottle so tipsy. The neighbor girl Kit claims we can play a game with this bottle, so we take turns carrying it home. It smuggles in my arms. We set it up on the sidewalk between two cracks. Kit spins it. The bottle points at me, impolite.

"Now what?" I wonder.

Kit says she doesn't have the answers to everything. She says I should have the answers to everything. I guess she's too young to know that her brain's healthier than mine. I don't tell her any different.

Her little brother Win is spying on us from the tree above. He calls us nasty, wild, kissy, and girl-on-neighbor. He says it makes him sick to look at us. Then he looks closer. He looks so close he falls out of the tree and opens his knees.

My father walks in from work and sees the knees. Their caps are off to us, or at least their flesh is.

"What's going on here?" Dad wants to know. And from

his bag he pulls a bottle of peroxide of his own special brand. He makes batches of it because I get in so much trouble that it's cheaper that way. He anoints the leaky wounds of Win. The wounds churn white foam and spit germs back into the world. Win bites his tongue to keep from crying. He skins his tongue on his teeth and cries some more.

"What happened?"

Win sniffles. He points to me, to Kit, to the bottle.

"It was an accident," I say.

"Accidents tend to happen," Dad says, "when there's drinking involved."

Kit tries to explain that we were only interested in the revolutions of the bottle, the uneven spin of its half-full body—

But Dad just takes up his peroxide and puts the lid on it.

"I've seen enough Kit. I think you kids should go home now."

After Kit helps her little brother up and into the building, my father takes up the bottle. He throws it against the ground to smash it. The bottle doesn't break because it's tougher than my father. He picks it up, strikes it against the tree, scares an apple off the branch. The apple falls far from the tree onto my father's head. He rubs his skull and sighs.

"After all you've been through," Dad sighs. "After all you've seen, I never thought you would take up drinking." Then he gives me my bottle back.

"Do the damage," he says. "Do it fast. Sometimes we have to do things in excess in order to get it out of our systems."

I ask him how I'm supposed to do a thing like that.

He straps me into his car and we bump off down the road, over to a shack thick with mousetraps. The whole place stinks of cheese. Between the mousetraps lady-drunks break heels flirting and flounce around on uneven gams. They lick the runs in their stockings to keep them from chasing up their thighs. When they don't have any spit left they pay men-drunks to lick the runs into submission instead. The men-drunks have spit to spare and get paid in shiny quarters. They put the quarters in the jukebox. This is why the songs never end.

"Kid's too young to be in here," shouts the bartender over the music.

"I'm trying to teach her a little lesson," Dad says. And he picks me up by the waist just like he did when I was small and he seats me on a stool.

"People need little lessons," concedes the bartender. He plunks two bottles down in front of us. Fruit rides their lips.

"But I don't drink," I tell my father.

"And after tonight you never will again."

"It makes me sick," I say.

"Sick is exactly how you'll feel," he says. "Tomorrow morning."

I explain to Dad that I don't want to be a drunk. I come from a long line of drunks mother-side, a lush people who inherited the least of the earth and curled up there. They were sponges with shakes, facefuls of veins awaiting a series of accidents who dangled cigarettes in bed and slept themselves into a crisp. They fell from roofs and lost their legs. They stepped on nails and locked their jaws. They made it so that when they died there wasn't too far to go. Just a minute from here to there. That meant blood ran cold and clocked.

"This will cure you of ever wanting to drink again," Dad says as he presses a bottle into my hands.

I tell him I'll look into it. But when I put my eye to the opening I see a froth hopping its way toward me and I don't want any part of it. I drop the bottle to the floor. It responds by smashing. Bubbles swill at me in threat. I hate those bubbles' guts. Their foamy hearts toil to burst. I like to break bubbles like they're blisters of woe.

"Now don't spill this one," Dad advises, handing me another bottle. He fastens my hand tight around its neck.

"I don't want to drink alone," I say.

"If you keep it up you will be alone. Everyone will leave you," he says, and he takes my bottle from me so he can have a swig for himself.

"Is that why you left her?"

He points the bottle at me. Then he drinks out of it. And goes back to pointing.

"Your mother left me," he says.

"That doesn't make it right," I tell him.

"Doesn't make what right?"

"You stopped looking for us."

"I still cried every night. That's a type of looking."

"It didn't do any good," I say.

"You came back, didn't you?"

"In part," I say.

He hoists his bottle up. He's only had a couple of draughts but already his tongue's gone to slur and over to stammer and back to slur again.

We take turns toasting by the light of the bottle, its frothy drink casting a luminous coma.

"To our health," Dad slurs.

I say something about going to bed now.

"To our happiness," Dad stammers.

I try to take his drink away.

But he keeps toasting:

"To the time when your mother and I first got together. It was at a party. She was wearing a bathing suit and eating an ice cream cone. And I threw her in the swimming pool. She got mad because she didn't want to get her ice cream wet. No, wait, it was her hair. Maybe it was her shoes. Now I remember. It was because she had a cast on her arm and the cast couldn't get damp. If it got damp all the information on it would go to shreds. And she had a lot of important information on that cast because she had troubles with her memory. Memos and things. Notes on how to get home. Reminders to pay rent. There was a phone number from a guy who could get her a job. He took pictures. You know? Of girls drinking soda through straws with lipstick on. And another thing was from her ex-boyfriend. Bastard couldn't even write. Just drew a bouquet on her arm. Supposed to be orchid. Looked like carnation. She started to cry. Said no one had ever given her flowers before. And now the flowers were gone. Everything was gone. She smacked me with her cast. Gave me a bloody nose. She wouldn't stop screaming. Said now she'd always be broken. She didn't have the money to get it fixed again. I told her I was studying to be a nurse. I drove her to my parents' house. People stared at us in the car because she was so pretty in her bathing suit. I took her into the garage and got out my saw. She closed one of her eyes. Squinted out the other. I sliced open her cast. I told her she didn't need that cast anymore. 'From now on,' I promised, 'I'll remember everything for you.' And when the plaster parted I saw her arm. It was pale and weak and childish. The fracture hadn't been healing properly. I had to reset the arm. I broke it again. I said, 'This is going to hurt.'"

   And this is the end of my father's toast because he's fallen off his stool and I have to hoist him up and hold him steady there. Holding my father steady is hard work and I have to do it alone. The men-drunks and lady-drunks would help me, I know they would. It's just not a good time for them right now. They're too busy setting their drinks on fire to keep their hands warm.

The next day my father overhears a bet between Kit and me. We're on the sidewalk watching flies gather on an abandoned hot dog. Kit puts five bucks on the fact that the flies will scatter when Win throws that rock at them. I double the bet. Win winds up. I get down on my knees for a closer look.

But my father's hand finds my ear. His fingers latch onto my earlobe and pull me away from the hot dog.

"So this is how you treat your money," he says. "No more allowance for you."

I tell him that this isn't my allowance because I already spent my allowance. Last week I spent it on a bet with Kit over what form the bruise from her mother's cooking spoon would take. Kit thought the bruise would be spoon-like. I wagered that it would be a dice-shaped injury, rolling high and blue on her cheek against the odds of a smile.

"And you lost, didn't you?"

I inform him that no one wins when there's a kid being marked.

"No more bets," he says. "Gambling is a bad habit with you."

I explain to Dad that gambling is only bad for me if I lose, and there's no way I can lose because if I know anything I know the business of flies. The people I come from have been working with them for generations. We're insiders on the habits of the low. Those flies act like they have it all, what with their diseases and innumerable eyes, but all they really want is to pile their eggs in the trashiest of nests. A fly wouldn't give' up fancy hot dog digs just like that.

But Dad doesn't listen because he's too busy strapping me into the car again.

"You want to gamble? I'll show you what happens to gamblers."

And he drives us down to the racetrack. We get high seats and popcorn there. Everywhere, it's a sure thing. There's a perfecta of horses, a payoff of saddles, gangs of white backsides hoisting themselves into the air. Men and women kiss tickets, hug binoculars, cheer into their drinks; they're all hoping here, and for that reason, they're the happiest people I've ever seen. I tell Dad so.

"You just wait and see," he says.

And then a spotted horse darts the corner and overtakes a brown bolter. The hoping crowd is no longer so hopeful. Some get happier, they whistle and high their fives. Others hide in their hats. They put their binoculars away and try to sneak to the exits, but there are muscular people blocking the doors with their widths. They wear fearsome suits with large knuckles that crack in warning. At the sound of the cracking the losers whimper, offer up wedding rings, offer up watches. The muscular people sneeze on these offerings; they twist the arms of losers behind their backs and make them lick their shoes.

Alarmed by the sight of all this loss, I promise my father I won't make bets with Kit anymore. Already, I have felt the experience of licking a shoe. The shoe licked me back. Its tongue had gotten around a lot. I think it gave me a disease because my hide went raw and a fungus started walking all over me. But Dad is unmoved by this confession.

"You need to get gambling out of your system," he insists. He gives me some bills and shows me to a window.

I argue that there are so many better things I could do with this money. I could wave it in Kit's face. I could put it in my jacket and lose my jacket somewhere so some kid would find it, some kid who never got fancy lunches and maybe that kid could buy a block of cheese for himself and eat it in the cafeteria in front of the bullies. And wave it in their faces. Dad pretends to listen to me.

"You don't know how to value what you've got," he says to me, and then he makes me hand over my money to the man in the window. The man counts the money. Then he waves it in my face.

"Which horse?" the window man asks.

I tell Dad that I can't do this alone.

"You're going to be alone if you keep gambling the way you do," he says.

I ask the lady behind me how she's placing her bet.

"Nobody's Business," she says. "He's a classic champion."

I ask her companion if he wouldn't mind disclosing his pick.

"Over My Dead Body," he says. "Always comes first."

Neither of these horses sounds good to me. I ask the ticket man to let Dad go before me. I can't decide.

Dad knows what he wants.

"Love of My Life," he says.

The window man taps his fingers at me.

"You want me to pick for you?" he says.

"Sure."

"Fine," he says, and he hands me a ticket and winks.

"Patriarch," the ticket reads.

Dad and I wait for our race. We buy soda and nuts and talk about our chances. Horses assemble at the gate. I can see Patriarch from here. He doesn't look good with the sagging at the mane and the balding at the butt. He's saddled with too much. He's too old for this. Dad's horse is different. A winner. She tosses her braids and whinnies forth a blue ribbon of tongue.

"Isn't she beautiful?" Dad says to me.

A gun snorts at the gate.

Dad gets excited. Veins mount his forehead.

"Love of My Life," he shouts, "don't let me down now."

And his wager bellows around the track, hoof-light, muscle-ready, prancing out the kicky flash of her fancy shoes. My horse isn't doing so well. He kicks up a fine dust at the gate and brays. The jockey digs in his heel. The couple near me points at Patriarch's scabby knees and laughs.

"Don't make fun of him," I say. "He's doing the best that he can."

And then no one is laughing at my horse. They're too busy staring at my father.

"Love of My Life," my father yells, "you owe me. You owe me big. We could have it all again. You just have to try. I can't keep picking up after your mistakes just to have you stab me in the back and laugh. Let's not do the old stab-and-laugh again. I know you had it bad, Love of My Life. I know you were sick. But I got you off those poisons. I made you chicken soup. I put you in a house with a real bathtub. You used to lie in that bathtub all day. But I didn't care. I just went to work so we could live. And I helped you make a kid so maybe you'd feel like coming out of the bathroom once in awhile. But you didn't. So you and the kid played in the bathtub while I went to work. Then one day I looked the other way, just for one minute, and you both were gone. You took all my money. I guess it doesn't matter. You left me lonely and childless. I guess you had your reasons. You made a joke of me, Love Of My Life. I guess I'll live."

And then Dad turns to me, just as the end is near.

"I've had enough," he says.

"Don't you want to see her make it?"

He acts as if he can't hear me, as his horse's nose achieves a first place finish. A choke of roses curtseys around her neck while Dad's ticket accuses him of being a winner. He doesn't trust the feeling so much, but he cashes it in anyway.

"Have you learned your lesson now?"

"Not really," I say. "I mean, after all, you did win."

Dad tells me that we both lost, a long time ago, before we even knew that winning was an option.

"But you have all this money."

"I guess I do. What should we do with it?"

I suggest that maybe we should send Mom some flowers in jail. I think they let her have flowers in jail. We should send her a purple fondle of blooms so she can wear one in her hair like a new ear. It would hear how much we need her.

Dad's quiet.

"I have a better idea," he says, and then he takes us to the nearest bar, a genteel trough where hatted ladies bet on whether butter will melt in their mouths and the pianist pounds keys with a rabbit's foot and the bartender throws some salt over his shoulder that sidles into my father's eye. He doesn't notice because he's had too many at this point. He says put it on my tab. He says neat. He says drinks for everybody! I send mine back. There's a fly sneering in it. I warn that fly. I tell him he's just asking for punishment. I stir him with my finger. But he's not going anywhere, that dirty son. He's just doing it for attention. I should know.

Today I invite Kit over for a new game, one that I figure we could get in more trouble with. It's getting harder to get into trouble these days since Dad just sits by his bedroom window and pours. Kit and I cashed in his bottle collection. With the proceeds, we bought all the things Dad won't let me have because they're not good for me. Like a brace of soda and a big bat. We don't have enough money left for a ball so we use apples from the tree. Kit pitches to me. I swing.

"Hey, batter, batter, hey," yells Win.

I strike one.

Kit winds up.

I strike again. It feels foul.

"Hey batter," says Win. "Hey batter batter hey."

I swing once more. I concentrate on Dad's bedroom window.

"You're out!" says Win. And then he grabs the bat from me. He lobs an apple into the air and hits it. It sails through my Dad's window. He sticks his head out through the hole and shakes the apple at us.

"What's going on here?"

"We didn't mean to," says Win.

"It was an accident," says Kit.

"I'm not sorry," I say.

"You did this?"

"Yes sir."

Dad shines the apple on the lapel of his bathrobe.

"Get up here," he says.

And so I run up the stairs to our apartment, past the super and the mailman and the couple who just moved in, they tell me to slow down, take it easy. They say there's no hurry. But they don't know anything. Specifically, they don't know that I'm about to be punished by my father and that being punished by my father is something I can't live without, because it means that we get in his car and drive away and spend time together. I take the stairs two at a time. I wonder where my father and I will go now. I take the stairs three at a time. I trip and fall. But I make this work to my advantage. Because I fall in front of our apartment door and Dad opens the door and shoves me inside.

"Go stand in the corner." He bites the apple I sent him.

"That's all?"

He chews in reply.

I tell him that there's not much I can learn from that corner. I suggest that we go somewhere. We can get in the car. Maybe we can go to the museum. Maybe I can learn not to be so destructive there.

"I don't have time for this anymore," Dad says. "You just get worse. Everyday, you become more and more like your mother."

I tell him that it's even worse than he thinks. I stole that baseball bat. I stole it because I am a bad person.

"Are you lying to me?"

"That's right. I'm lying too. Terrible, isn't it?"

"You look too much like your mother when you lie."

"This is true," I confess.

"You can come out of your corner," he says, "when you don't look like her so much." He adjusts his bathrobe and goes into his bedroom. I stand in my corner and think. The corner is dim. If I close my eyes I can't see my hands. I figure a similar effect can be achieved with my face and a light switch.

So I go to my Dad's room and I turn off the light.

"Will you punish me now?" I ask. My voice is dark inside the room.

"Come back," he says, "when your voice doesn't sound like your mother's so much."

I go to the cupboard and drink some vinegar. It blisters my throat enough so that I can go back to my father's dark room.

"Please," I croak. I touch his arm.

"Come back," he says, "when you don't feel like her anymore."

I go to my closet and put on my sweater. Back in the dark room, I hug him to prove my itchy touch.

"That's better," he says.

I move closer to him and stroke the arm that isn't busy with a bottle.

"You smell like her," he says.

I croak to him that I don't. My mother smelled like a burning feather I once lit. Her scent was pillow fight and full of scorch, it flamed midair and queened over sheets.

"You're lying again. You smell like her. You smell sweet. You've been eating sweets again."

I explain to him that I haven't. I only had some vinegar today. That's all.

"You want to lie to me like that. Go ahead. Lie to me some more. Get it out of your system."

I explain that I don't want to lie to him. Not on purpose at least. I come from a line of honest mistakes, things said without thinking, words that popped out of people who were just getting by. They really thought they'd have the rent by Sunday. They truly believed they couldn't get people pregnant. But then the eviction notices came and the babies were birthed and they didn't believe in anything anymore so they couldn't even tell what was true and what wasn't.

"That's some excuse," Dad says.

"Fine," I say. "I'll lie. But only if you will too."

"Sure."

"Show me how it's done. Give me something to work with."

"For instance," he says. "I'm asleep right now. That's a lie. Now it's your turn."

"I hate spending time with you," I say.

"That's good," he says. "But we need more. Faster. Lie faster."

"I hate spending time with you so much."

"Something else, something different," he says. "Get it out of your system."

But my system is out of ideas.

"That's it," I say. I tell my father that I'm confused. I'm more accustomed to the kind of lie that slips out when I'm caught doing wrong. I'm not sure how to make a lie that wants to be false. He gives me more advice.

"Just say the exact opposite of the truth," he says.

So I say:

"The day my mother and I left you was the best day of my life. We had been planning it for weeks, but it was my idea. I told her that morning that you didn't deserve us. I spelled it out in my cereal. She agreed with me. The sentence tasted sweet. I began to choke on it. You ran to my side and shook the vowels out of me. Mom said that choking was a good move on my part. She said I'd have to create more distractions like that so we could leave quicker. So I wailed in the night to buy Mom time while you comforted me. I laughed at the stories you read to me so she could sneak around and pack our bags. All of this packing made me hungry again. Mom said that if I was hungry I'd better get used to it. I wept. Mom said that I had to choose between the fun of leaving you, or a future with cereal, because you were the only reason we got to eat. I couldn't answer her because I got distracted by my hands. They were dirty and I didn't like being a dirty baby. Mom said that I'd better get used to it, because where we were going we'd probably be dirty all the time and people would think of us as things rather than people. 'Are you ready to become things rather than people?' she asked. 'Like an umbrella?' I wondered. 'Not as pretty as that,' she said. 'Like a doorbell?' I asked. 'Not so useful,' she said. 'Think smaller, think dirtier, think lower.' I sucked my thumb and thought long and low. I couldn't think very well back then because my brain didn't pay me any mind, but it knew enough to know that anything was better than staying with my father. 'I'll take that chance,' I told Mom. And so we crept from the house. I didn't even think about saying goodbye—"

"Are you done yet?"

"I never want to lie again," I say.

"Good."

I start to ask him if I can have another punishment now but then I see that he's busy. I hand him a corner of the blanket so he can take care of the accumulations in his eyelashes. And I explain to him that sometimes we have to do things in excess in order to never do them again.

"Sob faster," I say.

SIX

I'm good at being below things, especially the table.

"Fired again?" Dad asks. He lifts the tablecloth to have a look at me.

"I quit."

"Fired? Again?"

"If you say so," I say.

In the past two weeks I've had three jobs. First, I had one at the hospital. Dad got me that one. I guess he thought I'd enjoy being around blood because I talk about it so much in my sleep. And I did. I enjoyed mopping up it up and showing it who was boss. I was boss. I didn't like its kind hanging around my floor. The doctors said that the surfaces were cleaner than ever when I was around. They said they could perform surgery on that floor and then see their scalpels in it if the surgery was successful. It was that clean. "Now, now," I said, and I probably blushed because their compliments embarrassed me and because their compliments were in my head. The truth is: no one really said anything to me. I also liked my hospital job because I got to eat lunch with Dad. In those days we took the same lunch hour and ate from one plate. Everyone saw that I was his daughter, and he'd have people ask me questions about the world so they could see what I knew. "Magnetic fields!" I'd answer. "Chlamydia!" "Persephone!" It was good for my dad to be proud of me.

But then one day in the cafeteria the x-ray technician parked her stare across from us. The x-ray technician was frightening since she could see right through me. I knew she could snap my bones in a flash, capture all my innards in a radiant seethe. So when she asked me a question I shook. She knew that the answer wasn't in my head, but she asked it anyway, just to prove to everyone how stupid I am. My father tried to whisper the answer to me but I was too busy kicking. First, I kicked the legs of the table, and then I kicked the legs of the x-ray technician. I bruised one of her shinbones. The tibia, I think. And I felt sorry for it later, when I realized that I could have just responded to her question by saying that yes, I was having a good day. Because in the end, that was the real answer, the only answer, even if I didn't know it at the time.

My second job was at an arcade where I mopped and vacuumed and presided over tin coins that stoked a mechanic glow. The place was a slottery of luck and skill and I took care of the whole bleating operation. I tested joysticks, organized pucks, polished the metal hand that clawed at stuffy wonders in a glass case. From my belt a great teeming of keys swung. The manager loved the way I kept the kids from winning too many prizes out of the glass case. "Now, now," I said, because I couldn't take all the credit for the children's losses. My brother would come and watch me at work because he was proud of the way I could get him free games. He'd bring me sandwiches at break. We'd sit and eat them inside the hull of a rocket that let a person blow up suns on their way to the moon.

These games were good for us and we played them till we got fingeraches. Mostly, we played the one about a little pinball being rescued from a life of degradation by the swift kick of a flipper. The ball batted around, from corner to nook to crevice. Past tiny pits of woe and fluorescent traps it sped. The ball did what people told it to because it was better off that way. At the end of its journey, when the ball was finally safe, the hell it traveled in lit up and shrieked. My brother held the high score. It was a great game and I thought everyone should be able to play it. If they couldn't afford it, I just used one of my special keys to give them a free game. I told them they could pay the arcade back whenever they had the money.

The manager overheard me. He took my vest away, my broom, my nametag. He gave the vest and the broom to a new employee. He threw the nametag out because my name looks funny. I picked it out of the dustbin. Sometimes, when I don't feel safe, I put my nametag on for protection. I figure that if anyone's going to hurt me, at least they won't be able to whisper bad words in my ear. They'll have no choice but to call me by my name. And I'll just pretend they're putting coins in me. I'll light myself up for them and shriek.

At my third job, the boss said that he didn't know who I thought I was, but that I sure didn't look like the pictures I sent him. I told him that the pictures were of my mother, a long time ago. I told him that I was a part of her. He said that I certainly wasn't the part of her that stuck out so beautifully. He called me knee-high, food-stamp, trailer-face. Then he asked if he could borrow a stick of gum. He blew leagues of pink and airy sacks that rose like blisters from his lips. The bubbles amused him at first, but then he tired of their sticky resurrections. He took the wad out of his mouth and affixed it to a luminous end that was passing us by. The girl attached to the end stuck her hand to the gum and cooed. She waggled, showing me a shy bruise on her skin. I liked the way the bruise hid under its powder and paint. It was making an effort to blend in. I figured that if a bruise could do that, so could I. I told the man I'd do anything he wanted. He let me mop and sweep the girls' dressing room backstage. I knew the bruise would be proud of me, the way I worked.

The girls went wild over how clean I kept the floor. They said it was clean enough to kiss and paraded their lips over it as proof. "Now, now girls," I said, because when they kissed the ground beneath my feet it just made more of a mess for me. Still, abundances of marks mouthed off down the tile. The girls just patted me on the head and left to dance. I made friends with their lipstick once in front of the mirror while they were too busy dancing to notice. Its name was Grins On My Pillow. It had an effect on my mouth. The effect was that my tongue didn't want to be in my mouth anymore. It wanted to be in a different mouth. So I put my tongue in the mouth of one of the girls. She was strung with tinsel atop her gams, had a laugh as spinnable as a carnival ride I once threw up on. She laughed at me. She said, "Knee-high, you should know better." I didn't know what was better but I knew that my tongue still wasn't pleased, that it didn't like being in two places at once. I took it out and left. My tongue and I never returned, we just went back and sat on the couch and spoke to my father.

"I quit," I say.

Dad says I'll feel better if I come out from under the table and take a walk with him. Outside, he tells me that when I was born he had great plans for me because I stuck my head up right away and the doctor said that only the bright ones do that. He also says that when we were separated he wasn't happy, and he suspects his absence may have affected the development of my sad behavior. At the curb, Dad asks for two cones and points to my favorite on the ice cream charts, the strawberry fiend. The ice cream man says that there's only one left. My father puts down two dollars and goes without. And we continue, my father and I, past the park, the newsstand, the schoolyard, all of them bannered with posters of the missing, pets and people whose pasty faces promised reward. When I was gone Dad used to come and look for me here, he'd take his lunch in front of the posters and stare. Now that I'm back he doesn't even glance in their direction, he just rounds the corner and takes me into the graveyard. We sit on a bench with doves scarred into its stone arms.

"When your grandfather came here—"

"Why do you call him that?"

"I'm trying to tell you a story. A story that has a lesson. Now do you want to hear the story or not?"

"Can't you just call him your father? Just once?"

"Fine. But only for the purposes of telling this story."

And my father goes on to say that when his father first came to this country he was a man with a plan and the plan involved not being starved to death or taking a shower or digging his own grave. He wasn't sure this plan was possible though, so he made a new one instead. The new plan was to make enough money so that if people tried to fence him in again he could make a quick escape with a blonde and live the rest of their days on an island, but the realization of this plan looked a long way off because he held his pants together with pins and ate scraps from the bakery he worked at. He slept here, in this graveyard, where no one would bother him because of the dead. By and by he saved up a little money, went to college, built some muscle, and met a blonde with hair thick as steaks. She had sorrows too, but she tried not to show it much. They married and honeymooned with a waterfall and he got a job he was good at and she had babies she was happy with and they ate well and danced even better and then the babies grew and left and they were alone together, but not too alone. Really, they had everything they ever wanted.

"What about the island?"

"You've lived in that house. You know exactly what that is."

"That was a good story," I say. And I pat him on the knee. Partly because my hand is sticky with ice cream and I need to wipe it off, but mostly because I want to show Dad that I like him.

"I'm glad you think so."

"I especially liked the part about the ghosts."

"What about the ghosts? There was no part about the ghosts."

"The part about where the ghosts came up to Dziadek and tried to convert him to another religion but Dziadek made them eat improper food so they shriveled up and died again."

"That never happened."

"It did. Dziadek told me."

"So you've already heard this before?"

"Yes. But I like to hear you tell it."

"Anyway," Dad sighs. "I think you get the point. You come from good people with good brains. You just need the ethic. You just need to try harder. Will you try for me just a little harder next time?"

"Always," I say.

At home, while my father sleeps, I pack up my things. I pack crackers and toothpaste and an encouraging book about an orphan who crossed a river and came into money. But I know I should travel only with the essentials so I put back the crackers and the toothpaste. I pin my nametag to my coat and go out the door and hop on my bicycle and then I realize that I forgot something, so I get off my bicycle and run back up and write my father a note that tells him that I'll be back. I just have to make something of myself first.

Plot by plot, the cemetery flowers fake an interest in being bright. But I won't lie down with the graves, no matter how cheery the epitaph or settled the dirt. Instead, I throw my coat on the bench and put my book beneath my head. I try to sleep. My roommates are loud. They like to stay up all night and moan. But these dead don't seem to have it so bad. And I tell them so. They get sun and visitors. They have roots. And now they have me. I'll tell them stories if they like, groom their grass, prune their shadows. Just for now though, I inform them, I have to get some sleep, because I have work to do tomorrow. The crib deaths hush and the suicides take note. There isn't a peep from the murdered. Not a complaint from the natural causes. The accidentals are harder to silence. They keep banging on their boxes and talking about how their band's going eternal. I plug my ears while they dirge a rusty and tuneless chorus, their sense of rhythm in an obvious state of decay. I ask them to keep it down. They mumble something about people today having no appreciation for the past. "Your sense of timing is terrible," I say. "Tell us about it," they hiss.

In the morning I go see my mother's old pimp, my former tutor. I want to know if he can get me a job at the school. I visit him at his office, this shack on the edge of the outfield. He burns romance-scented candles in there, has a massage table folded in the back.

"Do you have a résumé?"

I hand him a piece of paper.

"This isn't a résumé. This is a page from the television guide."

I tell him that I watched that one show every day and it taught me a lot of things. Like how to catch a coma or inherit amnesia while the people around me assemble tiny dynasties, inbreed by accident, make the worst of living well.

"Well, that's good," he says. "But I don't know if you're really qualified."

I tell him about all the cleaning jobs I ever had—the hospital, the arcade, the tasseled shakery of limberous women. I tell him that making things cleaner by getting dirty is all I've ever been good for.

"We're particular about who we hire here."

I tell him he owes me one. He shouldn't forget that.

"I've been paying for years. You should see the dreams I have."

I warn him that I know my way around the principal's office. I can tell.

"Fine then," he says, and he pulls out some bills from an old jelly jar. "If your conscience don't bother you none."

"Oh," I say. "That's too much."

And I pocket it all before leaving. It's the school's loss. I could've mowed those fields into lawns fit for sunsets. I could've mended those fences hooky-proof. But no one will ever know. How fine my flagpole. How slick my hall. All I can do is go back to my new home and dream of scraping spitballs from the girl's bathroom, scores of papery wads trembling at the approach of my hand.

Back at the graveyard, everyone has an idea what I should do with my money. Those who lived too long think I should buy myself something nice. Those who died too soon would prefer that I donate it to research. I don't listen to any of them. I toss my money down a hole for safekeeping. "What do you think you're doing?" the goners cry. I guess that hole is supposed to become a resting place. So I climb in after it. But then I can't get out. I'm too short for this grave, my arms won't reach. "You did it to yourself," someone says. "No one will save you now," says another. But I grab hold of a rock and drag myself up. "Now I know how it feels," I tell all those goners, and everyone laughs. They laugh so hard they start to cry and their tears loosen the dirt, making it easy for me to dig a new hole.

The next day I go to see my brother's girlfriend at her work-place. She's a pretty punk, a blue-haired scalper who shampoos all day in a thick of curl-flurries and bad bangs. When I speak to her she's knuckling over the cradle-cap of a kindergartner.

"I'm busy," she says. "What do you want?"

"I'd like to have a job here. I'd like you to get me one."

"This is a difficult business. People trust you with the part of their lives that involves their hair."

"I can take it."

"To be honest," she says. "I don't think you could do it."

"Ouch!" bleats the kindergartner.

"I could. I really could."

"There are scissors around," she points out. "Irons too. If you hurt anyone I'd be held responsible." She nods at the faucet. "Turn it up for me will you?"

"Who's talking about hurting anyone?" I ask. I turn the faucet. I turn it a little too far.

"It burns!" the kindergartner cries.

"If you don't get me a job here, I'll tell my brother you were mean to me," I say.

"When was I ever mean to you?"

"I'll tell him you called me trailer-face, food-stamp, knee-high—"

"He'll never believe you."

"And while you were calling me those things you were touching my behind."

"Why would I do that?"

"Because you wanted to show your power over me," I explain.

She flicks a washcloth in my direction.

"I need this job," I say. "I need to make money and prove myself to my father."

She rummages in the pocket of her apron. Her glove surfaces with bills and suds.

"Just take that," she says, "and go. Okay?"

That salon doesn't know what they're missing. I could've made those customers hold their heads high. I could've built better comb-overs, parted it down the middle, buzzed that cut. But now all I can do is think of what could have been, hair stranded between my fingertips near closing time.

On my way home from work I see a sign with a face on it. The face isn't like the other signage faces. It's not different because the eyes are so immature. Or even because the mouth limps at one corner. There's just something familiar about it. I tear it down and put it in my pocket. The dead have a look at it. They tell me that it's my face in the picture, and I don't believe them, but then they point out my name. It's printed at the bottom. They say that I don't look that bad in real life.

They say that someone must be looking for me. I don't listen because I'm too busy digging a new hole for my earnings. "Go home," the dead beg. I explain that I can't go home. I have to prove myself to my father. Eventually, when I have enough money I'll return to him and buy him all the things he ever wanted. But for now I have to stay here. "It's okay if I stay a little longer right?" I ask. They pretend not to hear me. They just turn to one another and inquire after the weather of each other's bones.

The next morning I go see a boy I once knew from the ju-venile hall. He runs a paper route ring. No one in town can get a paper route but through him. In his garage-office sit dozens of boyish citizens, high rollers and folders of the daily news, their palms mossy with print.

He presides behind his desk in a chair that goes round and round. He has the same old scar from back in the day. There it is, traveling over the bridge of his nose, landing just shy of his chronic pinkeye. I don't know why I'm surprised to see that the scar still lives. I can't help but stare at it while he interviews me.

"Familiar with a bicycle?" he asks.

"Yeah."

"Do you require corrective lenses or any other visual as-sistance?"

"No."

"Could you learn your way around a puddle?"

"Sure."

He swings his chair around in a full circle before answer-ing.

"I can't hire you. Because I just don't feel like it. Now get out."

He snaps a rubber band at me. He throws the funnies in my face.

"If you don't give me a job I'll tell."

"Tell who what?"

"I'll tell authorities about what you did to me in the facility."

"What did I do?" he asks.

"You remember."

"I don't. What did you have in mind? Did I spy on your booby? Burn initials in your side? Did I pee in your ponytail?"

"I think that was someone else," I say.

"Did I rub one off on your diary? Did I choke you when no one was looking? Did I put a bottle up you when someone was?"

"I can't really remember—I have to think."

But he doesn't give me time to think. He takes me by the arm and drags me across the room. Past paperboys and tire pumps and extra-extras underfoot.

"I'll tell you what I did to you," he says, and then he leans in and whispers it to me. He kisses my ear and shoves me out the door.

I ask him how he could have done such a terrible—

"Maybe I did," he says. "Maybe I didn't."

I get on my bike. I could've brought people the best news, flung it straight to their doorstep with an expert wrist. But I never wanted to deliver that paper anyway. It lies a lot. There are ads in that paper, big ads, little ads, boldfaced cons slinking down the column. They claim that people are wanted.

This is the first night that I don't have to dig any holes to make a deposit. But I dig one anyway, just so the dead don't catch on. I don't want them to know that I didn't make any money. I pat the dirt even on my fake bank. I tell them that I've just had a trying day at work, busy, busy, last minute, snafu, riffraff, what-have-you, and I need to relax. I pick up my book and sit on my bench. But I can't concentrate because they're whispering about me. They bet that I was fired. They wonder when I'm going to start paying rent. They advise me to go back to my father. I put my book down. "Someday I'll show you all," I say. And I will. I'll cruise up to the cemetery in a car with all the doors on and buy pansied wreaths for everyone. They roll over in their graves in response. The dearly departed say they could earn a better living than I ever will.

In the morning I go to a card game under a bridge with people drifting beneath it. The hearts are on the table there, the diamonds, the ace. But the table is less a table than the stomach-slab of a bum with a belchful sleep. And one of the hearts is missing. So we use a moldy valentine in its place. The valentine makes it hard to bluff. When that card's in your possession everyone knows your hand's just full of sentiment and lace. I keep getting dealt the valentine. The faces of the two people I play with loom more hopeful by the game. I raise them.

The player on my right is a woman who wears a nun's wimple and a fannery of second-hand nails. The scavenged thumb has palm trees on it, and the pinkie's jeweled. I keep peeking over her shoulder to get a look at what she holds.

"What bright claws you have," I say.

She draws her cards closer to her chest.

"All the better to scratch you with," she snarls.

To my left is a man who wears sunglasses on the half-lens. They look crushed and vulnerable. I keep looking for a reflection in the glasses.

"What pretty red eyes you wear," I say.

He slaps his cards down on the stomach-table.

"All the better to weep on you with," he spits.

Between these two players I lose big. But I don't fold. And I keep playing and lose bigger. I tell myself this is my strategy. I want to appear a loser so as to catch them off guard and win harder. I lose harder instead. The table beneath our hands awakes. The tabletop man shakes the chips from his belly button and demands a cut from the pot for the flatness he's provided. The players look at me, expectant. I owe. I need to throw down. I study the veins that protrude from the tabletop man's stomach as if they'll lead me to a better answer, but in the end, their blue trails lead me nowhere.

"I don't have it with me," I explain.

The gamblers decide that the tabletop man will escort me back to get the money. I invite them to come along too. It's not so nice a place as they have here, I admit to them, but it's safer I think. People don't bother you much at my place because they're afraid of the dead, I explain. And I suggest that we can sit up for a while there and tell each other stories. I know a good one about the time my grandfather fought off a work detail by getting dysentery. But they don't want to hear it. They're going to stay here and guard my bike instead. If they don't get the money they'll feed my spokes to the gutter. They'll tear the clap out of my bell and take the air out of the only things that keep me moving forward in life. That's what I have to look forward to, they warn, if I don't make good. The sunglasses man seats the wimple woman on the handlebars of the bike.

"Look," they cry. "No hands!"

Some people have all the luck.

I give the tabletop man a little tour of my place.

"This is my bench," I say. "This is where I sleep when I'm not working at one of my jobs or riding my bike. When I'm not sleeping I'm taking care of my garden."

"This is my garden," I say. "Really, it's not a garden. Really, it's more of a cemetery."

"This isn't my cemetery," I say. "But it's my bank. I keep my money here. I bury it for safekeeping."

"This is where I bury my money," I say. But it isn't there.

I root around in a family plot. I dig between the twins who didn't make it through their first day. I dig by the woman that brought them there, and by the man who outlived them all. He has a weathered tablet that blesses me. It says that those who lose things will be comforted.

But the tabletop has strange ideas of comfort. His fingers apply themselves to my earlobe. Now he's putting my left ear to the ground. He says he needs to sit down somewhere. So he sits on me. It isn't so bad being under him. A person can hear a lot of things from this position if they pay attention. I hear Bibles atrophy and flags fade and wedding rings fall from disappearing fingers. I hear rosaries count off and photographs face silver linings. Mostly I hear someone's watch timing out far below us. Its tick is weak, but I can still hear it, and I choose to listen to the watch instead of the tabletop man because I don't need sound to know what he's up to. He's rummaging through my business. He checks pockets but finds only crackers; he removes my shoe and finds a pebble. I have a band-aid hidden by my sock. It's a special edition band-aid; honey bears parade on it. But he doesn't think to look there. He unbuttons my coat instead, and from the cups of my undergarments he extracts two of my personal belongings. Really, they've never meant much to me, but I don't care to have them slobbered on like that. And the watch isn't looking to comfort me anymore. Its tick got clocked. It faded and stopped. Instead I hear the man calling me shameful words. My fingers search out the lapel of my coat. They find my nametag. I show it to the man so he won't have to call me those words anymore. He looks at my name for a while.

"Is that really how you spell it?" he asks.

"Do you have a better way of doing it?"

"With the *y* and the *i* and everything? Are you sure?"

I tell him I think I know my own name. Both of them.

The man rolls off of me.

"Last one starts with a *g* right?"

"Yes," I say, "*g*, but my grandfather changed it when he came over here because he thought—"

But the tabletop man doesn't want to hear my stories.

"There's a reward out for you, you know," he says.

I tell him that I saw all the signs. They predicted that the time would come when I'd have value.

"I'm turning you in," he tells me.

He puts my personal belongings back. He buttons my shirt. He spits on my face and cleans it with his palm.

"I want half," I say.

SEVEN

A woman calls, she says that my grandfather just walked in the door with a sharp instrument saluting from his chest. "My grandfather?" I ask. "Your grandmother too," the woman says, and so I take a bus to the hospital and I run up all the stairs, towards kids on crutches and women in slings, through halls of thick and smirky babies, past bodies explaining bodies to the morgue, over to the ward where the sick are becoming people and the people aren't alone. I find my grandparents. They're taking their medicine.

"Here," I say, "I brought you some flowers."

"That's a banana peel," Dziadek points out. "And a hairbrush."

Babcia reaches for me. Her breast is corsaged with gauze.

"Call the nurse," she says. "We need to put these in water."

Mistakes have been happening. They don't need diapers. Her hair is uncombed. He stinks of iodine. They sit bandaged in separate beds with bare feet, brief gowns, longer drips.

"Was it hurtful?" I ask Dziadek, and I play with his new bed. I make it go up and down by the button.

"Not for years," he says. "Not for hours of years and then it up and numbered my heart and gave it a bad tattoo and threw it in the snow. I realized my family was gone. I was the only one left. And the world, once again, became intentional."

"Not that," I say. "Not that, but this." And I run my hand above that stretch of chest where he'd carved a new allegiance, a patch of stitch surrounded by sag and tuft.

"Not for a minute or so," he says. "Not for a second after a minute and even then it felt like nothing. It didn't stab me in the back but it pierced me from the front, and my life, forever and ever, remained the same."

"What about you?" I ask my grandmother.

"You never visit anymore," she says.

I explain to her that some people really don't care to be chased with a shovel in the early hours of evening.

My grandmother takes my hand. She likes to take things that belong to me because it makes her feel nearer to my father.

"I was not wearing my eyeglasses," she apologizes.

"Where is my son?" Dziadek wants to know.

He's busy. He's always busy helping people.

"I know this," he says, and then he sighs and turns to the nurse, this cheery young vein-tapper, and tells her that this wasn't the person they were hoping for and if there could only be a moment of peace—

The nurse turns to me, her finger on the pulse of something faint but reliable. Her hand circles my wrist; she guides me to the door.

"You," she says, she smiles. "Wait."

But I can hear it all as I leave, scraped by curtains on the way out.

"On a scale of one to ten," the nurse asks my grandmother. "What is your pain now?"

"I loved to watch my son's hair grow as a child," she answers.

I go to the lobby and wait there with the others. They know they are important for their injuries. Some of them moan, but mostly a man with his thumb stumping in a bag full of ice, his thumb-start tipped with gauze.

He makes accidents and is a carrier of fantastic diseases. He uncrosses his legs and leaves the woman seated next to him with a huff. She's too busy painting lids on her eyes to see what he can offer. He sits down beside me, crosses his legs holy so his toes stroke some promise in time.

"What are you thinking about?" he asks.

I think I tell him I'm thinking about my family. I think I tell him so my tongue can do the thinking for me. Other parts of me are not so qualified.

"You're too short to be thinking about family so much," he says, and as he says it he hands me the bag so I can have a look. He thinks I need proof that attachments can be forsaken, but I'm so busy watching the hangnail wink that I don't notice that the right side isn't up until the flesh is out of the bag.

The thumb swims on the carpet, knuckle-strong against the weave.

I try to call my father. I need to hear him say what my mother used to say, which is: you're right, sometimes you can't find a vein but you can tie one off when you think no one's really looking and if no one really is you can keep it that way, the knot near, the flesh whiter, but I only get the machine with his voice and it doesn't really say anything. It only says, now we come to the easy part of your dull and lurid inheritance, please leave a message.

Outside, I'm signing this kid's cast. His mother keeps breaking his legs. Then she tells him not to tell the doctor. He's scared.

"You shouldn't be," I say. "She probably just doesn't want you to find out that you can't run too fast."

Thigh to toe, his left leg takes my signature, even though it can't breathe. I'm careful to write my old and real name, the one my parents gave me when they were still together, back when it seemed like a good idea to make sure their kid stood out. My friend's name is common and better, his mother was wise enough to know that something else would mark him sooner or later.

"It's not that she's not thinking of me," he reasons. "It's just that she can't think of anything but herself, the forest, and the trees. All the rain, all the layers."

He's a smart kid. His mother pulls up to the curb in a car that runs on hobo juice and solar lint. She steps out of its gloss and coos towards us. Her muscles whir beneath her leotard, her arms scheme toward his breakables.

"I want you to have this," he tells me as she's throwing him over her shoulder with a pat for his behind and a pinch for my own slaking cheek.

And it's only because he didn't give me anything that I know exactly what he means. I sit in his chair, watch the wheels announce a squeak.

I'm practicing my right turn when two men coast up on a motorcycle. The motorcycle has a sidecar containing a small body. The body leans so that one arm is outside the car, its painted hand dragging on the ground like bait. The men dismount in unison and hoist the body out of the car. One takes the shoulders, the other, feet, and they drop the body on the step. This woman has a face like hide-and-seek all grown up, and when she stirs she smiles, she offers me her breast, says it's so full of milk it's hurting her, but I want something higher, that crescent nesting cold and plastic at her ear. It corrects her hearing. I propose a trade. I propose it by propping her in my chair. She seems to like this. She watches me hook it over my ear and nods an approval. Then she stops nodding. Now she's busy. She's eating off her lower lip. She wants to see it dangle like a spare tongue. At least that's what she tells me.

"You shouldn't do that," I advise. And she tilts an ear so I repeat myself. I repeat myself again, and again, and once more.

"I'm trying to understand you," she says.

Even Dad doesn't know how to talk to me anymore.

"What's going on here?" he demands.

He's intimidated, I guess, by my new ear, which can hear so much better than the average ear, and more. I heard him coming. He came without flowers.

"You know very well what's going on here," I say. "Yesterday we were alive and safe in the old country and now we live in a land where our blood is going coastal, now it's low tide and we're all starting to recede…"

My ear now has another gift, in that I can no longer hear myself because I'm so busy turning the aid up to hear other people. Now it makes sense to me, how when people get really old and weak, they can live longer than anyone.

"I just got the message," Dad says. "What happened?"

"I guess they were trying to dig something out of their chests. I guess that's what they were trying to do."

"Out of their chests?" he asks.

We wait for the doors to open and then we're running into the hall. I lapse and bruise myself; I trip over a therapy dog.

"Hey!" the receptionist says. "Watch it!" And she gestures to our handicaps with longing and disgust, because she's the one in charge here, she's the one keeping it together, and it's hard not to envy us. We're the ones with the privilege of falling open so our wants writhe like germs in season.

Past the curtain my grandparents are eating bowls of soup and watching a program on how to tie your shoes. This instruction is achieved through song and dance, as led by a hedgehog. There are lots of closeups about knots. Every time a knot is made the little animals bleat with joy and rub their fangs. My grandparents love to see problems solved too. When their son enters they clap their hands and weep.

"Who shot them?"

"No one shot them," the doctor says. "At least no one I'm aware of."

"I'm a nurse," Dad says.

"Well then," the doctor says. "Well then, you know."

"I could," Dad says, "but I don't think I do."

The doctor informs us about the incident. That there were hesitation marks, but nothing was superficial. It was planned, noted, it was meant to last forever.

My father looks to his parents.

"Who wants to die!" Dziadek exclaims. "I never heard of such a thing."

"We just wanted to see you," Babcia explains.

"How else were we supposed to see you?" they whisper.

The doctor says we look like we could use a moment. And so his white coat turns and leaves with the rattle of his instruments, minus one hammer. His distraction made it easy to pocket. I make my leg leap out at the knee.

"Good for you," Babcia says to the reflex, but the rest of the room remains unimpressed.

"We're taking you home now," Dad says.

"Of course," Dziadek says. "We will just do some swinging by our place first for articles of a personal nature."

"Yes," Babcia agrees. "We cannot sleep without our boots."

"No," Dad says, "I'm taking you home. To your television guide and fig tree and mailman and doorbell and gardener. To your telephones and your hot tub. To your closets stocked with enough canned goods to get you by when the world decides to end again."

"We will stay here then," says Babcia.

At least, I think she's the one who says that. But it could be me, because my mouth is open.

"What good can come of you staying here?"

"Cheaper than a hotel," Dziadek says.

"Not really."

"Cheaper than a hotel," he says, "and people will help you to the toilet too."

"I'm not arguing with you. This is one thing we're not going to argue about."

Dziadek removes two rings from his left hand. He gives them to my grandmother. He flexes his fingers, sifts the joints, grips the bed rails. My father lunges for him, he picks up Dziadek and the old man's gown gapes wider even than his mouth. No one wants to witness this, but there it is, it's there, an aging nudity dangling in a disinfected room.

"You never broke my heart," he hisses. "You never stabbed it once and stomped on it in your stocking feet and tossed it out a tall building. You never tied it to a stone and sank it to a river bottom so it would shrivel smaller than your soul. You never did that, because others did it before you had the chance. They did it by turning my heart to meaty soap back there, all those years ago. At least they were making me feel something when they did it. Come now, make me feel something. You were never dead to me. You never died and lived again, as a meat-lamp, as a meat-soap, because you were born here, raised here, as they say. You are here and still I never see you because you are not dead, you are just living here, away from me, and I feel nothing. Come now, make something of yourself. Show me what you're made of."

And Dziadek pounds the stitches on his shorn chest.

My father closes his eyes.

"Papa," he says. "I can see everything."

"What is this you see? You don't see anything. Esther, what is he talking about?"

My father opens one eye, just enough to squint through, just enough to see where he's going. He steps toward Dziadek and fastens his gown shut with a jaunty knot.

"That's better," he says, and my grandparents don't disagree with him, they just look at my father and then they look at me, but nobody speaks, no one says a thing. We're too busy listening, all of us together, to the sound of a man being extinguished in the hall, his body hosting some random flame.

EIGHT

All the white-capped little swimmers make waves. They do the scissors and the butterfly, they sink and crown. Here, at the community pool, I work as a lifeguard. I save people from rowdy splashes and chases around the deep end, and on occasion I can be relied upon to breathe my breath into their mouths without kissing them. My only interest is in those kids making it another day to swim some more, to hit that high dive, to tuck that somersault. In return I get children spraying their lung juices all over me, a sweet acid wafted from overwhelmed organs that follows my skin around until closing. On the bike ride home, I always count the lives I've saved on two crossed fingers that uncross back and forth. At least, that's how the day usually ends, but today, as I lock up, I see something happen in the parking lot. It changes things.

In a car there's a man whose scalp is sliding off his head. His golden wig is struggling to leave him. He keeps trying to readjust it while talking to a tiny girl with wings made of water. The wig-man is trying to give her some candy, some cherry kid-stuff that gleams sugar-heavy in his palm, but she won't take it, she says no thank you, and bobs her bathing cap. Then the wig-man tells her that he's looking for a lost little boy, and he wonders if this nice girl would be willing to look with him. Having overheard this, I can't help but go up to the wig-man and tell him that I know about lost children. I ask him what this lost boy is like.

"He's just a boy," the man says, and he gestures with his hands so the candy falls from them. "Just, you know, a boy?"

"Is he this tall?" I ask, and demonstrate that I can use hand gestures too. "Or that smart?"

"That tall."

"This wide? That Mexican?"

"Maybe. It's been awhile," he says.

And this is when I get a better look at the man while he sweats. There's something unbalanced about him. It's probably just his eyebrows. They're crooked, drawn on with shaky hand. He seems to need to keep his shaky hands busy at all times, and he achieves this by clutching at his wig and taking shots of his inhaler. He sucks air back like there isn't enough to go around for all of us.

"I know exactly who you're looking for," I say, but he drives off before I have a chance to tell him where my brother is. I guess he had to go somewhere. I guess he had to hurry up and buy lots of toys so my brother will forgive him for leaving. If he'd waited I could've told him that my brother doesn't play so much with toys anymore. He'll be back though, that man. I can tell by the way he looked at us as he drove away, one eye peeping through the rug sliding off his head. He watched that little girl and me as we got down on our hands and knees on the pavement. We had to pick up that candy before someone else beat us to it.

Even the diving board is acting jumpy. We're all in wait for something today. The kids queue up at the bathroom. They leap from foot to foot and grasp their swollen parts with shriveled fingers. Their mothers turn on towels outside cannonball range; they rotate themselves in oil and burn to a fine crinkle. Lizards shade and lose their tails to the kids that hunt them. It's a long wait, this wait for the wig-man. I don't know how long it really is. I only know that my whistle keeps whistling louder and my ladder keeps getting higher and more dirty words are appearing on the shower walls. The words say that I blew it. I don't know how everyone figured out my secret, how they learned that I lost my brother's father once again. The sun keeps beating down on me but I don't hit back. It has the higher ground, I can see that. The children let their bladders prank in my pool but I don't yell at them. They're in too deep to know better. The mothers wade and compare tans and question my credentials. I tell them they can think what they want of me but I'll never stab anyone in the tonsils with a knife, because that would be as wrong as anything else, like breathing the same air as they do, or calling them ma'am. The mothers scowl at me and leash their children tighter.

At the end of the day I climb off my perch and pound the water out of an albino. This is when I see the wig-man again. There's his car strolling up, that smoky gleam of metal with the kind of windows that only see out. At the curb, he invites a small boy in a cap to look at a magazine with him. He's teaching the boy to read with women as words. The nice women are attached to their bodies, to cuddles of bones and rashers of flesh. Shivers travel up their spines. Even though I like to look at the women I get angry at the sight of this lesson. I don't understand how this man can justify taking the time to give some stranger boy a reading lesson when once, long ago, my brother and I were left to teach each other with the words off a can of beans. We schooled out the rules round the garbage can. We went one bean, string bean, red bean, green bean while this guy was probably off working miracles with the phonics of other children's mouths.

The boy in the cap panics when he sees me running up to the car. I've had this effect on many children since becoming a lifeguard. I tell him it's okay, he's a good kid, he hasn't been peeing in the pool, he hasn't been jumping in the shallow end. But his greasy back turns and runs.

The man panics, slams his door. The magazine flutters on the sidewalk and the man starts to roll up the window but I stick my hand in there.

"I know who you are," I say. But he doesn't want to hear about how he's the father of my brother, the father of a boy he left to fend for himself in a worldful of claws and cold fires and rotten meat. So he pushes my hand away and takes off down the street. I figure I can't blame the man. I can only follow him.

There's an address on the magazine and a name. Or there was a name once. Now the print just says "Mr." and a smudge. The magazine leads me to a neighborhood where people glare over their rosebushes for recreation. An eye for every bloom they stare, swish their clippers, yank thorns and children from their sides.

I go over to help the kid up.

"Don't touch him!" the mother cries, and she pulls her child close, so close he starts to choke, and she gives me a look with her eyes, that look that says I'm not welcome around here, so I slink across the street, towards the man's address, where things have suddenly become warmer, and full of light.

There's something burning on the doorstep.

I ring the bell. Mr. Smudge answers it wordlessly in a rug of curls, his mouth occupied with a glass of orange juice.

"There's something on your doorstep," I say. "And it's burning."

"What do you want me to do about it?" he asks.

"Maybe you could pour some of your juice on it?"

"No."

"Do you have—I don't know—maybe some hoses or something?"

"Not really."

"Fine then," I say. "I guess you and I will just have to do this by myself."

And I stamp out the fire. I put out the doormat but my pant leg gets sparks all over it. Little flames lisp over the weave.

"Can I come in?"

"Maybe when you're not so much on fire," he says.

"Not even to use the sink?"

"Look," he says, and his thumb indicates the clutter of a lair behind him. "I've got a lot of valuables in there. I don't need them getting scorched. Or looked at."

I ask the man just what I'm supposed to do then.

"Just as they say," he shrugs.

So I go over to the lawn for the stop, drop, and roll.

"Be careful with that lawn," he warns. "That grass has been around since my childhood. That grass and I grew up together."

I stop and I drop on the lawn, roll once, roll twice. The fire likes my leg. Its intentions are good. It only wants to keep me warm, but I extinguish it still.

"Now can I come in? I just want to talk to you for a minute."

"No. I'm busy-busy."

"Did you know your nose is bleeding?"

It's true. Drops quartet above his lips.

"Not again," he says, and he starts to wheeze.

"That's no way to make friends," I say.

"I'll say. But what can you do?"

"I guess you could blow it."

"I don't like touching it."

"No one does."

"Will you do it?" he asks. "Please?"

And then he opens the door.

Inside, Mr. Smudge has a lot of things that I can't touch. He says that most of them are left over from when his mother died. His mother loved cough syrup, I guess. The coffee table has crowds of bottles tall and squat and lit from within, a sluggish glow piercing amber innards.

"Keep your head back," I say. I have him prone, his throat laid out over the back of the couch. I hold the tissue with one hand and drink cough syrup with the other.

"How much longer?" he asks, his voice pinched and high.

I tell him it'll be just a little longer. The bleeding stopped a while ago but I prefer him like this. He's a better person with a tissue interrupting his face.

"Are we done yet?"

I take the spattered tissue away.

"You should really wash your hands now," he says.

I go to the bathroom.

"Be careful with that soap," he yells after me. "She used to wash my mouth out with that soap. I grew up with that soap."

I open a cupboard in the bathroom for a towel. That's when I see the checkered sadness Mr. Smudge has accumulated. It's heaping with Monopoly and all the other games, the this-and-that trap, the Clue, the Life. A kaleidoscope that lets you see beaded depictions of boredom when you turn it. A bear that professes a monotone love when you punch his abdomen. The toys are new and wrapper-fresh, ready for pretend, for spare time, for those hours I've always heard about, after dinner, before bed, that a kid's supposed to spend being a kid.

"What's taking so long?" Mr. Smudge shouts.

I could ask him the same question. About how he collected all these toys for my brother over the years and never gave them to him. But I figure there's always time for that. For now I'll just go out into the living room, I'll sit across from him in the plush chair that looms so high that my feet can't even touch the floor, and I'll swing them back and forth, back and forth, until I don't feel like swinging them anymore, or until Mr. Smudge tells me to stop being such a child. Whichever comes first.

At work the next day, I'm distracted. All I can think about is how much my brother would've liked to get his hands on those toys. They would've come in useful whenever he needed to be distracted while we were growing up. I could've cheated him at checkers, shortchanged him at Monopoly, toppled his dominos. I could've given him something else to cry about. But it's too late for that now. Now, I just sit back and watch the children amble poolside. They've got rubber glasses that let their eyes see without sting. They've got caps to keep their hair from green, towels to dry their corners, lunches to get sick on. These kids don't even have to lift a finger to plug their noses. Clips do that. The clips hang on necklaces round their necks. Alongside whistles and lockets with portraits of parents grinning descendant grins. Closest to their bodies, these kids have everything a kid could want, maybe even everything some adults could want too.

Today there's something dying on the doorstep. I've come back to ask Mr. Smudge why he let my brother down, but the dying distracts me. So does the neighborhood watch in the yard across the street, a parental unit staked out on the lawn with binoculars while their kids turn cartwheels. They're yelling at me to get away from that evil neighbor. The parental unit says that their neighbor doesn't deserve any friends, and their kids agree with them. The kids run into the house when the man comes out of his; they stick their mouths to the windowpanes and blow onto the glass, their exhalations shaping themselves into a cloud of warning.

"What do you want?" Mr. Smudge demands.

I point to the dying. I go to pick it up. I explain to him that we have to give that old possum a proper burial.

"Don't touch him! He belongs to me."

"I saw him first."

"It's my house," Mr. Smudge says. "And I don't like you touching my things. That possum grew up here, just like me. We have something in common that you don't. He's mine."

So I watch as he hikes the possum up by the tail and carries it inside the house, past a wall of cuckoo clocks with birds all chimed out, through the parlor gone to sun and doily, into the hallway where his mother's rouged face and lazy eye preside over a tear in the wallpaper. I put the tear there the other day, coaxed it with my teeth just to see if he would notice. But he moves right past it with complaint only for the kitchen, which he says stinks of sickness but smells to me more like killing pain with spoonfuls of jam and pills. We don't disagree over this for long though because as soon as we're outside the house we're busy disagreeing about something else. He says that the backyard resembles an overgrown disaster, but to me it looks more like a good place for a dead possum to be dead, just another anonymous goner afield. Mr. Smudge gives me a shovel. He takes the possum from me, lays it belly-up, and this is how the possum becomes a girl to us, because rows of breasts rouse beneath the fur.

"That means there were children," he says, and I make my shovel bite the ground and dig a young dent. I swing away at the dirt. It makes me feel good to scare those worms out and create a tender grave. Mr. Smudge rests the possum there, he tweaks her eyes shut, coils her tail neat, and then the dirt blankets her body until there's nothing left, not even a whisker. I start to say a prayer over her but Mr. Smudge says that prayers are curses when they come from the filthy. He says I'd better go inside and wash away as much of myself as possible.

In the bathroom, I attend to my blistered hands. They're done in by sores, a fester for every fingerprint. I try to make one hand wash the other, but the soap stings so much that I have to hold it with my mouth. Between my lips the soap bubbles. That's why my brother's name sounds so clean when I go out into the living room and speak to Mr. Smudge.

"What does he look like?" he asks me. He offers me baloney and three kinds of cough syrup on a silver platter.

I pull the picture from my pocket, the one I always carry. It's of me and my brother, when we were small and in the habit of taking baths together.

"And who's the little girl?"

I'm too busy to answer him since I'm eating. I'm chewing and swallowing and the soap is starting to taste like baloney and the baloney is starting to taste like it needs a little cough syrup. Fortunately, Mr. Smudge drops the subject. He moves on to other, more important things.

"Tell me more about your brother."

"I think he'll like you."

"What's not to like?"

"You can be mean."

"Besides that."

"You're also bossy."

"But other than that."

"Your hair is falling off again."

His fingers search his head. When he feels only skull he starts to squeal.

"Don't touch me!" he says when I try to help.

But I can't just sit there and not do anything about it. Again, I try to fasten that little wig to his scalp, but I'm not even sure that I want to try. He seems like a nicer person without his hair. Just a moment ago he was balding and we were having a nice conversation, and now he's smacking me.

"Stop touching me," he scolds as he smacks. "I don't like your touching."

And he follows this protest up with a curse so loud his nose starts to bleed.

"But you're sick," I say.

"There's nothing I can do about that."

"You need help."

"I've tried getting help. It doesn't work."

"Let me help you," I say.

So we sit awhile. He slaps his wig on crooked and I reach to straighten it.

"Don't touch that," he says. "That's made of my mother's hair. I grew up around that hair. I used to brush it in my child-hood. Every night. Sixty strokes."

So I look at him instead.

"Don't look at me," he says. "That's just like touching. But with eyes."

So I sit beside him instead.

"Don't sit there," he says. "If you sit there you might as well be sitting on my lap and if you were sitting on my lap we'd be touching."

I realize what I must do with myself in order to be near Mr. Smudge. I go to the toy closet and I shut myself up there and I grow a little younger. This makes me a better person. As proof of how small I can be I recite the alphabet. My insides organize accordingly. They go from appendix to bowel to coccyx to duodenum to esophagus to gallbladder to hindbrain. I say my numbers too. There are five entrances to my senses and two to my body, which are private parts. Those parts are in my pants, they're going undercover, they're going to find out what I have to do around here to get some respect. What I have to do to grow up and be a real girl who doesn't have to be little in order to be good.

He knocks on the door.

"Is everything okay in there?"

And that's when I know everything is. I only have to prove that I'm good by not keeping Mr. Smudge to myself. I have to introduce him to my brother.

But I don't say anything about this at the moment. For the moment, I only tell him that I enjoy the dark.

"That's nice," he says. "But keep your hands to yourself. I grew up with that darkness. That darkness is mine."

The next morning, at the pool, I think about how nice it would be to teach my new friend how to swim. He'll look great in a pair of goggles and a neon bathing cap. He'll need a bright cap to fancy up his scalp, something to make up for the absence of his curls. Free of his wig, he'll be a far better person. He'll be shy around the chlorine at first but we'll start at the shallow end, where the littler ones have tea parties in the clear, and then we'll move a few strokes deeper, to the four foot mark where there's lots of kids, their bodies ballooned by all that swallowed water, and Mr. Smudge will probably cling to me there, because the pool is so choppy, so full of bugs and backwash, but we'll keep going, on to the deep where the bigger kids dive for quarters and he'll call heads and I'll call tails but in the end we'll both be winners because he'll have learned the breaststroke and I'll have been the one who taught him. It'll be what they call a win-win situation, and I'll dry his head off in the sunlight, buff it to a shine so high and beaming that all the kids can gather round and see their faces in it.

After work I go over to the house again. He's invited me this time, says he'd like to hear more about my brother. I sink into the couch and watch commercials with my feet up.

"Don't put your feet up!" he says. He brings me a shiny platter of baloney and three kinds of cough syrup.

The commercial I'm watching is about a boat that'll sink if you don't eat your oatmeal. I don't understand what it means, so I ask Mr. Smudge.

"Don't ask with your mouth full," he says.

I start to drowse. I can't see anything. My eyelids are in the way.

"Don't fall asleep," he says.

And just then there's a knock at the door.

"Quick!" he says. "Hide!" And he shoves me into a closet.

I hear a man with a twitchy footstep walk in. I bet he's leaving mud all over the floor, and I bet I'll have to clean that mud up later. I realize that I haven't known Mr. Smudge for very long, but I'd just assumed I was his only friend. This other friend is my competition, I guess. Maybe that's why Mr. Smudge wants me to hide. It's dark here, in the closet, and full of coats that smell like wet candy and rubber doorbells. The coats grope over my skin. I guess my hand is sticking out beneath the closet door because my host puts his shoe over it to cover it up. This is when I realize that he's embarrassed to be seen with me because I'm filthy and full of cough syrup. My person is disorganized, shuffled, unfit to be seen. Even my undergarments show, they slip and strap and put me in a bind. They say I'm not a kid anymore. They say I should grow up. I hear the visiting man leave, and as his door closes I open mine. This is when I ask the question, the one that's been bothering me for a long time now, from the very beginning, when I first met the wig-man, my brother's father, and tried to take him as my friend.

"Are you embarrassed to be seen with me?"

He says he isn't sure what I mean. He reclines in a huff on the couch and sucks at his inhaler.

"I mean, are you ashamed to have me around? Is there something about me that's so bad that I don't even know about it?"

"Why would you think that?"

"You never take me anywhere," I say. "And you don't introduce your friends to me."

"That was my parole officer. My parole officer only wants to know me."

"You were in jail?"

He mutters. About crowded showers working him into a lather. About tin plates and tinny bitches and Bibles that see red, lawyers in exodus, great pillars of saltpeter, a lights out, a lockdown.

"My mother's in jail. Did you see her?"

"I'm afraid not."

"Did she talk about me?"

"Like I said—I didn't see her."

"Oh."

"Is that why your neighbors don't like you? Because you were in jail?"

"I guess you could say they think I have no decency."

"You keep your house really clean though."

"They should leave me alone. I've already lost everything—my mother, my job, my friends, my future—"

"You're all out of baloney too," I tell him, and then he excuses himself and throws up in the bathroom and I hear him in there, retching into the toilet, and I think about going to help him but I get distracted by what I'm seeing out the window instead.

There's a teenage boy out there with a can of paint and a brush. The boy dips the brush into the paint and leaves letters on the side of the house. He leaves them red on white and five feet tall and runs out of the yard. I go out front to have a look. I'm familiar with the word. It starts with a *p*, it has four vowels in it, and it sounds like love but really, it just means that Mr. Smudge is someone that can't be cured but can only be punished. It means he's not my brother's father, just a different kind of worse. Sort of like a person who blows smoke up kids' belly buttons, melts their snowflakes, leaves them under ladders, hides their pants on picture day, tears the daylight out of their homework, and then, after all that, makes them cry and critiques the weight of their tears, the red of their eyes, the screwy aspect of their wailing face. But worse. Mr. Smudge comes out and shakes his head at the word. He starts to gasp for air like he always does in his most anxious moments. I put my arm around him. I tell him that my brother and I will come to his house after I get off work tomorrow and we'll cover that word up together, we'll make it like none of this ever happened. We'll make everything right, I tell him, my fingers crossed behind his back.

Under the sun at work, I plan how to get back at Mr. Smudge. These kids that I'll save, they'll thank me. They'll bring me snack cakes poolside and wash my feet with their ponytails. They'll paint my nails pink and pledge their lives to me. I won't want any of it. I'll point out that it was just a matter of humming some wind into their throats, just a deal where my shadow kept their skins from burning, only a lark where sickos were bayed from hanking their pankies around smaller-bodied persons like themselves, pastless kids with insides empty as their cookie jars. It's what anyone else, I'll say, what anyone else who was me or my brother or maybe even a few other people, would do.

I don't even have to ring the doorbell this time. It's the day of the event and I've arrived early, sudden moves dancing in my head, fingers ready to carry them out.

"How do I look?" Mr. Smudge wants to know.

He looks like a person who has problems. He's got eye-sacks and fidget lip. Cotton perches in his nostrils for the sake of the latest bleed.

"Do you like my shirt?"

"I think a suit might be overdoing it."

"What if I don't wear a tie? How about that? Is that okay? Or maybe—if I do wear a tie—how about this one? Will your brother like it? It has cartoon characters on it, like on the television, see?"

He makes a knot.

"How about this knot? Is this knot okay?"

The knot doesn't offend me so much as it makes me feel like a loose end, it makes me not want to pull through on this plan, not keep myself together. I think about how my own father doesn't take such care with his appearance for me. My father shrugs around in workout shorts and old karate belts. If we're eating any animals at dinner, he'll wear a shirt for respect. He'll wear a shirt with a palm tree on it, and afterwards, he'll wear a towel to the shower. Sometimes the towel will be striped, sometimes, just yellow. It makes me wonder if his love for me is really so great. Maybe Mr. Smudge's love isn't so terrible after all because he dresses up for it and he buys things and—

"Don't just stand there like an idiot in the doorway," he yells.

But I can't fool myself into believing he'd be a good father. He makes me think about things that I'd rather not. Like certain facts. Like how, sometimes, when you become an adult, you're no longer a child. You put away your childish things until you have nothing left, and that's when you start hurting people, that's when you start stabbing them in the back and telling them they're down in the mouth, because there's nothing like fighting with nothing to make a person feel alive, except for maybe, touching them where they don't want to be touched.

"When is he getting here?"

"He'll be here," I say. "Just wait. Just see."

"He was supposed to be here ten minutes ago."

"He'll be here," I say. "You just have to be patient."

We wait in the parlor. Mr. Smudge isn't good at waiting, he's too anxious. He keeps crooking the portraits straight on their nails. He shuffles books on the coffee table in order of smartness. He rearranges the candy bars he keeps under the couch cushions, lines them up in order of their sweetness. He peers out the window, careful to keep his face hidden by the drapes.

"When is he going to get here?"

"Soon," I say. "Why don't you put on some music? You know, to pass the time?"

So he puts on music, changes tunes, makes the radio jump from oldie to top ten and back. Then he seems to think better of it. He puts on music suited to the process of getting to know someone. A piano scales high and low. There are no words for it.

"Is he here yet?" Mr. Smudge asks. "When is he going to get here?"

I look out the window.

"He's here," I say. "He's coming up the drive on his bicycle."

"Do I look okay? How do I look?"

"Your hair's sticking up."

He moves to adjust it.

"Here? Right here you mean?"

"No," I say. "Over there. It's sticking up right there."

"Here? You mean here?"

"No," I say. "You're getting it all wrong. And you don't have much time to get it right. He's getting off his bicycle now. He's chaining it to the post already."

"That means he'll be at the door soon," says Mr. Smudge.

"That's exactly what that means."

"Here," he says. "You fix it. And hurry."

He offers his head to me. I run my hand through his mother's hair, inspect the place where his rug meets his neck, that soft spot that might be the only good spot on him, and I pull his second scalp away from him, I hold it high in my hands and jump on the couch, and he's crying for me to give it back, he's trying to snatch it away from me, but I'm too quick for him.

"Is this what you want?" I ask him, and he nods his barren head. I reach out to hand him the wig. I snatch it back when his grasp gets too close. I offer it to him. I take it away. Now he's got it. Now he doesn't.

"Is this what you're looking for?" I say, and he begs for it, but it's hard for him to reach with one hand when he's so busy covering his scalp with both. He ventures a finger forward. I put the wig behind me.

"Guess which hand?" I say. And he guesses left, no right, no left, but none of it matters anyway because I'm tearing the hair out of it, and together we're watching it fall, by the strand and the tangle, by furl, by thread, until there's nothing but a pile on the floor for him to rub his face into and a barren cap between my hands, just a flap of skin with nothing to hide.

"Please," Mr. Smudge says. At least I think that's what he's saying. I can hardly tell, he gasps so much while he's lying there choking on a lack of air, with his mouth going blue and his chest heaving, and I could lean in to help him, I could part his lips and slip some oxygen his way, but instead I run my hands across his glassy curios, his antique lamp, his rosy piggy bank.

"I'm touching your things," I inform him.

I palm the white queen of his chess set. I knuckle a piano key. I thumb through the gold leaf of the family photo album. While he gasps I finger the velvet buttons of his ottoman, rub a cheek against the nap of his curtain, tug a stray thread from its hem that measures the distance between his kind and mine. It isn't much.

"I'm touching your things," I say, and I keep touching, late into the night, until all is said and done and touched.

NINE

When I go back it's because they have nice doors and those doors are the only things I feel like touching right now. I go back during visiting hours. The nurses putter in their whites, check the screens that border their outpost. They don't recognize me, at first. I'm not as lined with slits as I once was. I pull from my pocket a piece of chalk, which I carry by way of identification.

The head nurse nods. We used to be great friends. She'd liked the way my hair fell over my face so she didn't really have to look at me.

"How are you?"

"I'm learning how to drive."

"Good for you," she says. "That's the kind of thing we like to hear about. People learning."

"I was just driving by. You know, just driving."

"It's a nice day for driving."

"Yes," I say. "Driving. Learning."

"So. What can I do for you?"

"Well," I say, "I'm afraid my car broke down. Or maybe I ran over something. Maybe it was a dove. I have a feeling it was a dove."

"Are you alright?"

"Yes, I just—I was wondering if I could sit awhile."

"Of course," she says, and she gestures to the waiting room.

"No, I mean. In there."

She doesn't say anything. Other nurses drift past, their hands filled with pills, with vials, their own sad faces spilling nothing by way of news or meaning.

"I have friends in there," I say.

She pauses but my insides don't, they keep nesting with each other's jokes. They wink and call out to me. They want to know if we're there yet.

The nurse glances around. She wants someone to help her.

"Why don't you just have a seat?"

"If you insist," I say. But mostly I say it to myself.

I see parties of families going in. They seem happy to be there. The head nurse writes their names out on nametags so they can become visitors, there, on the other side of the door, but to begin with they're family. They cross themselves, surrender sharp objects, bear fruit.

"Is it because I didn't bring anything?" I ask. "Is that why you won't let me in?"

"That could be a reason if I was looking for a reason," the nurse says. "But I don't need another reason. Now, am I right or am I right?"

The nurse addresses this question not to me but to the giant who guards the whole place. He's this badged sentry, a grey colossus with a club hulking at his side. He glances up from chewing on his nails to answer her.

"You're right," the giant says.

"They're still my friends," I say. "It doesn't matter whether I'm in there or not. They're still mine. I mean, you're my friend still right? So come on, let me see."

She shakes her head.

"Let me see the twitcher, okay? Just, just five minutes. That's all."

"I can't do that."

"Can I see—"

"No," she says.

"What about that guy with the leg? You know, the one who did that thing with the car and the lake?"

"Oh—you mean?"

"Yeah," I say. "Come on, let me see him."

"No. Not happening. Not possible."

And then two more visitors trot up. They both wear high white socks and cheap haircuts but only one of them is a dog. The one that's a dog smiles at me and unfurls a polite tongue. The nurse buzzes the door open, and when I ask her why a dog can go inside but not people like me, she pauses. She gives my question a lot of thought and so her answer accumulates considerable volume waiting in her brain. I hear her too clearly when she finally speaks.

"Because he makes people feel good," the nurse answers.

"I can make people feel good too," I tell her. Her look for me is skeptical.

"Here," the man with the dog says to me. "I'll show you." And he takes my hand and he moves it over the dog, he shows me how to stroke in one direction so the fur lies flat and thick against my palm. It's true. I do feel good. All the things that keep me from keeping well fall away and I'm intact. The dog nuzzles my shoe. He's only an animal but even he knows it's safe to be kind to me. I try to return his kindness with a vow.

"I swear I will give you," I promise the dog, "all the things I never had, and some of the things I did, except the stutter, except the lice. And if ever you're living in a barrel making men squirt for coins and cops are pulling your hair out and schoolchildren are lobbing their spit at you and clinics claim your brain is moot and your mother, somewhere, is building a small nativity, something with bottle caps, a manger full of dirty spoons, I'll sink my teeth into people for you. I'll folly them deep into skins who suffer less for your weakness. And our life together will be a series of streets where they like us and streets where they don't, tails that will be lucky and heads that won't, bones that'll break and bones that won't, but as long as I have you to rest my arms around everything will be fine, I swear—"

"That's enough now," the nurse says.

So that's how this relationship ends, the one between the good feelings and me. The man takes the dog by the leash and leads him through the doors; I go back and sit by a plant that's busy starving. Leaves flag as a fly rubs its feet together, buzzing over us all.

"What's the matter?" the nurse asks.

"I'm in pain."

"Where does it hurt?"

I know it hurts wherever they took the dog away from me but I don't really know where that is, so I come up with the next best place.

"In my shoes," I say.

"Maybe you need a new pair then."

"They are kind of busted aren't they?"

"Hmmm."

"Kind of down around the lace?"

"If you say so."

"I have an idea."

"Does it have anything to do with being quiet?" the nurse wants to know.

"No."

"What then?"

"It's about you giving me a pair of those slippers. You know, standard issue?"

"Okay," she says. "But only because you look so good in them."

She cups a hand to the giant's ear and whispers to him. Then she takes out a key, and I watch her white uniform retreat to the supply closet.

When the last of her disappears round the corner, I creep up to the countertop. I want to see the kids who were my friends. But I'll settle for the ones who weren't. I put my neck out for them; I stretch to see down that hallway. I'll take a glance at any of those hazy madcappers that reason quit—the stitched and the sorry, the last-chanced, sulkers and sleepers all—the whole pack of them drawing straws as short as their memories are long. If I can't see the whole of their bodies I'll settle for pieces of them. Just the dartle of an eye at a keyhole. Or the briefest peep of feet beneath the window drapes. Any indication, that's what I'll take. Any indication that they still are.

"If you don't get down from there, I'll have to remove you," the giant warns.

"Do you know any of my friends?"

"Get down now."

"You've got to know the one with the lumps. You know, the one who always did that thing with the weather forecast and his head?"

"Please remove yourself."

"Everyone knows him. Everyone knows that guy."

"Well, you can't see him anymore," the giant says. "Now get down from there."

I'm confused and I tell the giant so. Am I not good enough to see him? Is that it? Is the weather guy so cured now that I can't see him anymore? I swear I'm good enough now. I can get letters of reference from my neighbor Kit and my father to prove it.

"Doesn't matter how good you are," the giant says. "Only way you can see him is if you're up there—" he thrusts a meaty pointer at the ceiling.

I think I know what he's getting at.

"You mean he's in the rec room? Playing ping-pong?"

The giant huffs a little, starts to speak. But the nurse comes back before he can yell at me.

"Quiet Earl," she snaps. And then she says to me, she says, "That's right, he's playing ping-pong."

"Good," I say. "He needs practice. I'm tired of having to be a winner."

The nurse leads me to my chair and takes my shoes off for me. Like old times.

"Who's he playing with?"

"Playing who what?" She's distracted, I guess, by my shoelace system. My knottage technique is something that I'm still working on.

"Who's he playing with?"

"Oh. I think...that other boy."

"Which one? That runt with the crossed eyes? The lisper who liked music therapy too much?"

"Sure," she says, "that one."

"That's good. I didn't think he'd ever—"

"A remarkable recovery," she says, and she says it so I can't interrupt her. She holds up the slippers.

"Now," she says, "if I give you these, you have to promise something. Again."

"Anything."

"Promise you'll never come back here again?"

I promise to stay out as easily as I've promised it once before, and so many times before that. To nurses and nuns and elevator boys. To bus drivers and Ferris wheel operators and bunny handlers at the pet store. The tattoo parlor had me put it in writing. The butcher shop wanted it in blood. My mother never wanted it at all. I gave her my word anyway. It was cold but open to interpretation. I gave it to her because my hands were full. I needed to free one up so I could turn the doorknob and leave that room because her boyfriend was killing us both. Slowly, and with a bottle full of snow. But I'm not proud of that promise, even if it's the only one I've ever kept. This one's new, different. I promise the nurse that I won't be back.

"Good," she says, and she slips the slippers on my feet. They have grins stamped on the toes. She goes back to her files. I sit and watch the grins waggle on my feet. Then I watch the giant watch me. The nurse doesn't watch me. She's busy at her work. Over her files she whistles one of the old music therapy tunes, some little ditty about a sunny side of the street. I try to whistle too. I put my lips together and glow. I feel brighter, but the sound doesn't happen. I figure whistling might just be one of those things that comes with work.

"I think I need a job," I say.

"I agree. Then you could get shoes that aren't made of paper."

"It'd keep me feeling good. It'd keep me feeling like I have a purpose."

"You'd be occupied," she points out. "You'd be too busy to keep coming around here all the time. Every Wednesday.

Bothering me during visiting hours. That's always important."

"I always thought that if I had a real job I wouldn't get into
trouble so much."

"You're right on that one."

"But sometimes I also think that the world's full of cloud-
mongers and they keep dropping pianos on my head and they
keep telling me it's rain, they keep telling me it's snow—"

"That's just because you're not taking your medication."

"Would you like to give it to me?"

"I'm not authorized."

"Can you give me a job then?"

"We don't have any positions open."

I tell her that there's no job too small for me. I have skills.
I can stitch kids up in there, I can help them remember their
names and build their birdhouses. I can stand watch over their
beds as they sleep. I can help them cheat at bingo, wet their
lips, convince them they haven't really gone albino, no matter
how much their mind says that even their color has abandoned
them.

"You need to go home. I'm going to call your guardians, if
you don't go home."

"I don't have any guardians. I'm too old for guardians remember? You kicked me out because I got too old for everyone."

"Listen," the nurse says, and she clutches me by the chin.
"You just can't come around here anymore. It's not like you get
anything out of it. What makes you come back?"

I answer by telling her what she already knows, which is
that once she brought me a cake and then she kicked me out.
The cake didn't have candles on it but it said that I should be
happy. It said it in red sugar. That was something. I wanted

to eat that whole cake by myself. I wanted to slice it down its jellied center and show it who was sweet. But the nurses made me share it with the other kids. They made me share it with my grandparents too. That was the most frightful sharing I've ever done. Since cake gives old people powers. It made my grand-parents strong. They ate and ate, and then they said it was time for us to be going. They laid their hands on me. I tried to hide beneath the nurse's skirt. Below there it was voluminous and cool. I figured this shelter could summer me through to an-other season, until I was better prepared to face the world. No one needed to know. I would lodge my toothbrush in her waist-band. I would hang my pictures from the runs in her stockings. I would read by the light of her pale and radiant kneecap. I could pay my keep by making sure her slip never showed. But my grandparents dragged me from her with their cake-muscle until the nurse's hem tore and she was left there in her undergar-ments. She was so sad to see me go with a piece of her skirt in my hand. She hit the wall and wailed. I could hear her as we left. And then she cried some more, for days and days, but I couldn't comfort her. I couldn't even hear her because I was gone, I had left her all alone because my grandparents put me in their car. They gave me the strap there, for safety's sake, and buckled it in. Then we drove over the train tracks where two pennies awaited a certain doom. The drive was bumpy, my head hit the ceiling of the car, and the life we moved toward was one that I didn't care for so much, because it had no warning in it. That life was built to rise and shake out my insides, it was happening, it was final, and there was no way to scare the cure back in me.

"Do you remember it?" I ask the nurse.

"Not like that."

"I think I left something behind here," I say. "I think I really did."

"Well," she says, "if you left anything it'd be in here."

To me she hands over the lost-and-found box. According to this box, someone out there is going through life without their glasses. Someone else is managing without their bloody mittens. That can't do them any good. Another person has been separated from a plastic case. Inside the case, bedded in tissue, is a translucent canopy. I've seen these things before when I was in school. Rich kids had them to make the roofs of their mouths brighter. I dangle this finery on my finger from a loop of wire.

"Can I have this?"

"Is it yours?"

"It sure is sticky."

"But does it belong to you?"

I think about this for a moment. I wonder if all these things belong to the same person. This person must be wandering around with bad vision and chapped hands, the roof of their mouth naked and ordinary. All of this sounds familiar. I wonder if it's me. There's only one way to be sure. I pop that red canopy in my mouth. It crackles, shifts. It's too fancy for me and it won't hinge with my jaw.

The nurse shakes her head.

"It's not what I'm looking for," I tell her.

She takes the box and tries to shoo me out. There's no arguing with her. I figure I'll just have to show her by my actions. As proof of my good intentions I take out my belt and the pin in my hair, I make myself more harmless than anyone could ask of me and it looks like she's considering it, it looks like I might be getting through, and then I notice the monitor, it's trained on solitary and I lose all interest in going in, which is to say, I see what I came for.

There's a kid girl in there. Lying on her stomach with her

hands folded beneath her head. She's wearing my old sweater. I put my hand out at her. Just a touch to the screen. I like to poke girls to see if they're done yet.

"She's still here?" I ask.

Once, I sold my urine. I sold it for a match. It was coveted, my urine. It got me out of those detox classes all those other kids had to take. It got me far. The match was brunette. It was about to fall in love with the side of a matchbox but then I realized its full currency and traded it. I could have traded it for anything. But I bought something instead. It had felt good to be the buyer for once.

That girl in solitary, I knew her as Hannah.

Once, she was interested in what I had to offer. We had a deal. She led me down to the quiet room one evening. She sat me down, she stood before me. Her hips swung. She knew what she was doing. We didn't have any music so I hummed. She told me to stop humming so I did, and after a while I forgot and started humming again, but by that time she didn't really care, she was too busy dancing and I thought about dancing too, just for a moment, but then I changed my mind because that wasn't really what I was paying for. She danced because I paid her and she danced because no one could hurt us again because only children hurt and we weren't that anymore, we were something else, but what that is I don't know because she's inside and I'm out here and my hair keeps falling in my face, it won't stay out of my eyes, I think I need to get it cut.

TEN

Moses thinks the genes are closing in. It's his birthday. I could give him something he wants or something I want for him. Like a telescope or a day at the movies with me. I haven't decided yet. When I was his age I was in the hospital. This is only on my mind because he's asking me about it right now.

"When'd you start having problems?" he asks.

"With screaming? As long as I can remember, but then I learned how to eat sugar so I couldn't feel a beating—"

"Not that problem. Your other problem."

"With the uterine cotton? Not until I was seventeen."

"That's not what—"

"And you're a boy. You don't have to deal with that. You have to deal with other things. Like your voice changing. And that should be happening any day now."

"That's not what I'm talking about."

"You might think that's not what you're talking about, but really, you're talking about it every time you speak. We can all hear that your voice is high."

"I'm talking about the hospital."

"It's not such a bad place."

"But they lock you up."

"It's not such a bad place."

"They take away your belt so your pants fall down and you can't even use a fork or take a shower without someone watching you. You sit around all day yelling at the radio about undergarments and peeling a banana. And then you attack a nurse because your gut says she's got a gun and they haul you off to crisp your brain."

"How do you know?"

"There are films," he says.

"Made by filmmakers," I point out.

"Plus I visited you once."

"I don't remember."

"I'm not surprised. You were pretty doped up."

I wonder what it was like when my brother visited me. I would've liked to have known he was there. We could've made my bed together, teased the pill bottles, counted stitches in the arms of easy chairs. I bet it would've been a good day. Almost as good as this one's going to be. But my brother has different ideas about what it takes to make a good time.

"It must be hard," he says.

"What's hard?"

"Going through life interrupted by thoughts that interfere with your living."

"There are ways to live around thoughts," I tell him.

"Show me," he says.

So I take him to the roller rink and we put on skates. I do an expert gimp-maker. My brother performs a triple black eye. He lands that landing. All the little girls applaud in pastel.

Past us they twitch, padded at their girl-parts, their shifty skirts lifting. I had underwear like that, once. Their panties are calendared, cut French, printed rosebud. They're bow-tied and crotchful, churchy at the pelvis and pruded at the mount. The panties are connected to legs and the legs are connected to wheels. When hundreds of wheels are connected to girls with money and faces they are called a taunt. This is my understanding at least. The taunt of wheels goes round and back again. The girls get in giggle formation. They clasp waists and trail into each other so quick that they become only a flash of hair-ribbon and a peek of kneesocks. The taunt of girls claps and spins and glides past on those rubber wheels. I push my legs out faster so I can be closer to the wheels, so I can hear what they're squeaking through their axles. It's just as I suspected. The wheels claim that I'll never be fast enough. Too much of my brain, they squeak, is given over to gnawing itself through a scant livery of chemicals. I'll never catch up. I am too slow. In my brain's defense, I take out one of the little girls, the one whose wheels squeak loudest, with a tug on her ponytail. She falls, and the girl before her falls, and the girl before that, and around the rink girls upturn until all the wheels flurry in the air.

"That's one way," I say.

My brother takes me to a beach for another try. At the beach I see bathers burning, but they don't seem to mind the sting, they just put their cigarettes out in sea shells while muscle bounders flex oily flesh at the horizon. Beneath umbrellas, Boy Scouts consult binoculars about the profiles of breast feeders and honeymooners grow dusky husks. Babies catch sand in their diapers and give the sand to castles. A bottle washes up on shore. I open the bottle and see something stirring inside it. I drink the bottle so my brother can't drink it.

There's poison in there, I figure. Better me than him, I figure. And my brother's already sleeping. He's belly-up with a book behind his head while I have a thought. The thought says that the tide is turning. It says that I have to protect my brother from the oncoming surf so I heap sand over him. My brother's neck loves the sand. It wants it higher and higher. I notice that the more I bury my brother, the more the sun disappears. I pile sand on my brother's neck so the sun will go down faster. I want it to be dark so we can go to the drive-in and watch a movie. You can't watch movies in the daylight there because the jokes are only funny in the dark. That's my understanding, at least. I pile my brother's chin with sand. His face is surrounded. A crab scrambles from a nearby shell. I guess the crab doesn't like how the shell speaks to him, so I put it to my ear for a listen. The shell says that someone's put a taste for the horrible in my mind in order to convert my soul. I don't know what's so bad about that. But then the shell starts to scream. It screams so loud it wakes my brother. He sputters because his mouth is full of sand.

"That's another way," I say.

Moses grits his teeth.

"This can't be the way to go about things," he says.

"Prove it," I say.

Moses thinks we should meet with a number of experts to advise us on our options concerning the impending lack of sanity that is our familial inheritance. I say this is no way to spend his birthday but he insists. First we go to a fortune-teller, a woman covered in veils above the laundromat. We hand over our palms.

She informs us that this line on my brother's palm is love and this one is fate and they join a little at an angle that indicates luck, so that's good, that's okay, but this one here, this line, the one with the break in it? That line ends in crazy.

"Now you," she says to me, leaving my brother to stare at the diagram of a doomed future.

I give her my hand.

"How about a different one?" she says. "One that's not so covered in sand?"

I give her another hand. She recoils at its jammy surface.

"I can't work under these conditions," she spits.

So my brother's crazy palm leads me into the bathroom and turns the sink faucet to a drip. I cup my hands for the water and scuff them on a bar of black soap. My brother helps me rub my hands together. But they won't come clean. Marks stay on them. Smears too. The soap gleams blacker in my hands. It curdles and darkens, casts a foaming shadow. It escapes me.

My brother stoops to find the soap. He slips and falls instead. He hits his head on the side of the bathtub.

"Are you hurt?" I ask. His eyelids are wavering.

"No. But I'm seeing things."

"Nasty little points of light that shiver at the crotch?"

"That's it."

"Those are stars."

"That's what they want me to think," he says, and he tries to crawl out the bathroom window but only half of him makes it through.

"Help me," he cries, and he's still crying for help even as I pull his body back indoors, even as I drag him past the fortune-teller's grasping veils, even as I deliver him out the door and onto the street, its curbs agleam with the freshest red paint.

"You kids have no future!" the fortune-teller yells from her window.

After the fortune-teller's, we go to a therapist, this soft-spoken guy who wears sandals in a room full of teapots. He encourages us to talk about ourselves, to make ourselves comfortable, to lean on that pillow over there. He wants to hear our dreams.

Moses speaks about a dream where he was in a phone booth with an individual who kept trying to make disturbing calls to our mother. The individual kept asking Moses, how do you like that? And Moses never knew whether that was meant for our mother, or for himself, but he figured it was probably for himself since every time that statement was made the individual twisted the knifepoint against his skin.

"And what about you?" the therapist asks me. "What are your dreams?"

I tell him I'd like to take care of myself someday, like a real person.

My brother draws close to my ear.

"Your nightmares—talk about your nightmares."

"No," I say. "I can't do that. Someone might be listening."

But my brother gives me a look that means I have to try for his sake.

So I talk about going to the school dance and spying the girl who said she was mine latched to the arm of the kid who beat me in the spelling bee. The winning word was one I had never encountered before, but it meant loss. Even worse, at the dance, the spelling bee winner and the girl were rubbing their parts together during our song. Still worse, our song is a long song.

"And when they were, as you say, rubbing parts—how did you feel?"

"I'm not sure."

"Did you feel a sense of panic? Like something had been taken from you?"

"Panic. Yes."

My brother raises his hand. As we've been instructed to do before speaking.

"Yes, Moses?"

"That's not a real nightmare."

"Moses," the therapist says. "Let's not invalidate her consciousness."

"But it's not a nightmare. She's just making stuff up."

"It happened," I say.

"Yes," Moses says. "It happened. It happened to me two weeks ago."

"So it seems that your sister has a problem with living through other people?"

"No. The problem is that she lives through me."

"Is this true?" the therapist asks.

I tell the therapist that I once dreamt that I was in a phone booth at the park with this simple little boy who loved his mother too much. I kept calling the mother and asking her to pick us up but she said she was too busy so I said how do you like that? And I kept saying that over and over because it made it easier to stick the boy with my knife when I said it, and sticking the boy with my knife was the best I could do. Sticking the boy made the flowers outside the phone booth grow faster. It mended sidewalk cracks, let the traffic lights go green, kept the anthills from being stomped on. As long as I kept sticking the boy everything was good because the mother would feel like she had to come and save the boy from people like me.

"And what does that dream mean to you?"

I tell the therapist it probably doesn't mean anything since it's not a dream. It really happened. I explain to him how most things that happen don't mean anything because they're too busy being real.

"Why did you do that?" Moses wants to know.

"It hurt me more than it hurt you."

"But she came and picked me up?"

"Sure she did. She always did when I pulled that one."

"So it's all just my memory?"

"Does that change things?" I ask, but I can tell from the slack in his jaw that I'm not really going to get the answer I want to hear.

"It's not a dream. It's just a memory," my brother mutters to himself, and he gets up from his pillow and walks out of the room, leaving the therapist and me to stare at the banging door.

"You kids should get some better memories," says the therapist.

The pastor at my brother's church is eating cookies out of a cookie jar embossed with a crown of thorns. He gives my brother a cookie. I can't eat one since I'm sitting on my hands. The pastor says I have to because that cross on his desk isn't for touching.

"Now what can I do for you two?"

My brother explains. That we'd both like to be upright. That a life spent in alleys, on wards, behind bars, is a life we'd like to avoid, but we fear that this is something that runs in the family, and we've heard that the things that run in the family are the easiest to catch.

"You should pray," the pastor advises, sopping his cookie in a glass and shaking it at us. Sacred tears of milk sermon down my blouse.

"We do pray," my brother says.

"You should clean your hearts and then pray."

"We do clean. Then pray."

"Pray harder."

"We're cleaning and praying as hard as we can."

"Help the needy. And pray more."

"I help the needy," my brother says. "I wash my next door neighbor's car. He has arthritis, vertigo, high blood pressure, anemia—"

"And what about you?" the pastor asks me.

I tell him I write letters to our mother.

"Then you kids should help the hungry too. Then pray."

I tell him our mother isn't hungry. She gets oatmeal in jail. And napkins.

The pastor frowns. He brushes crumbs from his collar. Then he gets up and shows us the door.

"I thought you were helping us," says Moses.

"I am helping you," the pastor says. "I'm helping you help the needy. Because the needy need my help more than you do. So by leaving right now, you're helping me have more time to help them. See?"

And then he shows us the door. It isn't much to see. Just a brace of splinters on the hinge. But when he swings it open my brother clings to me.

"I hear voices," Moses says. "Terrible, squawking, clamors of voices. Sickening, awful, rasps of voices."

He buries his face in my coat. I plug his ears with my fingers till we're safely past the choir room and its crowd of robed followers with their holy mouthing, their voices a petition to madden the nearest sinner.

"You kids couldn't lift a prayer to save your souls," the choir sings.

So we go to Dad. When he sees us at the door he retreats to the bedroom to put on a nicer bathrobe because he still considers Moses company. Then he goes back to making my vitamins in the kitchen, organizing colors into a supply luminous enough to cradle my organs for a month. When he pauses to evaluate the distribution of these chalky substances, we take the opportunity to talk to him. We explain to him that we want to know the source of this. If we can know the source of my illness, my brother reasons, we can deal with it better.

"Not from my side," Dad says.

"That leaves her," nods my brother.

Dad sifts grain into tiny capsules. I take Moses behind the refrigerator door for a meeting.

"He's lying," I whisper.

"Why would he lie?"

"It's just something he likes to do. From time to time. Like when I drew a picture of a lamb. He told me that I could do better."

"What should we do?"

I think back to my time in the hospital where people were in the business of knowing who among them was sick. But all I can think about is the first night there. A man watched me as I slept. I knew he was watching because I was really awake. It was hard to sleep with all those applications being made to my arm. First, a needle plunged. Then a tiny jar bubbled with red and the man carted it down to the lab where white coats held it up to the light and deduced my genetic misgivings from its contents. That was how everyone learned that something in me had gone wrong.

"This is what we do," I say, and I tell my brother the story of the jar.

"How are we supposed to get that?"

I take out my pocketknife, which was entrusted to me by our mother. It has sparrows on the handle and I know she'd like my brother to have it. She told me so while an apple fell in half. She told me that the knife was capable of only good, but my brother is suspicious of the blade.

"Will it hurt him?"

I consider this: in the hospital there was only hot and cold or soft or sharp or sturdy. I don't remember feeling much of anything when the needle plunged.

"Of course not," I say. And we go back into the kitchen.

"What did you kids do today?"

I tell Dad we went to the music store to try on woodwinds because Moses needs a new one. We didn't get in any trouble, I tell him.

"You wouldn't be lying about that would you?"

"Why would I lie?"

"Sometimes," Dad sighs, "it just seems like you enjoy it."

He segregates his capsules. The empties pill near powdered bullets.

"What's this one for?"

"Keeps your liver shiny."

"What about this one?"

"Makes your kidneys hum."

"Are you sure that's for my kidneys?"

"Sure I'm sure."

"But the one I've been taking is yellow."

"That is yellow."

"Is it? Seems like saffron to me. Maybe you should look more closely."

Dad lowers his head to the table to inspect the vitamins. His lowered head leaves behind a band of neck, pierce-ready at the collar. And my brother sees that this is his chance. He tips the knifepoint into the back of the neck. The blade doesn't have much going for it. It leaves only a scratch and a bead.

But Dad can feel it.

"What do you think you're doing?" he yelps.

My brother doesn't even try to take the sample. He just pockets the knife and runs. I hear him wrestle with the door-knob on the way out. From the kitchen window we watch him kick a tree and push an old lady and catch a bus.

"Something's wrong with that boy," Dad says. He shakes his head and pushes a collection of gut shiners towards me.

I take those vitamins because I'm going to need all the strength I can get. My brother is gone. I figure it'll take a phone call to find him.

When I get to the park I see that my brother's not the only one waiting for answers. At the phone booth there are a couple of runaways, kissy teenagers who keep strangling each other to make their faces go brighter. They get the hush from a bare-chested old man in floral pants trying to apply chap-stick to his lips with an ashen claw. He purses and misses and purses again, leaving trails of wax to course from ear to ear like glossy erasures. Behind him there's a barefoot woman with her face lodged between white headphones; she sways back and forth in the mud, mouths the unheard into a muddled lyric. My brother is the last of these people. He shifts from foot to foot, twitches with a couple of bottles tucked into his pants and a blanket thrown over his shoulders. He doesn't look any differ-ent from the rest of the people gathered here.

In this dark the phone calls out to us. The floral man an-swers.

"Uh huh, uh huh," says the floral man. "Yeah. So. And?"

Then he passes the phone to me.

"For me?" I say. Sure enough, it is. When I put it to my ear the phone shrieks that I'll never be enough. It takes low, ragged breaths, brays about darkness. It wants to supply fires with me, it wants to know if I like to swallow....

I hang that phone up.

"What did it have to say?" asks the lady with the head-phones.

"It says we just have to wait a little longer," I say. "Just a little longer, and then we'll all have a reason to be happy."

The teenagers paw each other in celebration. The lady of the headphones and the floral man hug. But my brother only glares at me.

"You shouldn't lie to us like that," he says. "It doesn't do anyone any good." He takes a long swig from his bottle, longer than usual, just to prove his point.

"Did you steal that?"

He sucks in reply.

"That's terrible. Can I have one?"

He lets me help myself.

"Thank you," I say. And when he shrugs his shoulders at me I see there's a blanket around them.

"You stole that too?"

He grunts from behind his bottle.

"It smells terrible. Can we share?"

He puts one corner of the blanket around me.

"Thanks. I'm sorry I don't really have anything left to give to you."

He pulls the knife out of his pocket.

"You already gave it," he says to me. And then he and the blade huddle over his arm. I snatch it away from him.

"I want it back," I say.

"It's mine."

"Mom gave it to me first."

"But it's my birthday," he says, and he wraps his hand

around the blade's end.

"Let go."

He doesn't. He just waggles his fingers around the edge.

"Hey, just let go and I'll get you something nice," I say. "Whatever you want. For your birthday."

His hand holds fast.

"How about a haircut?" I say. "A judo tutor? A coupon for the lottery?"

In spite of all these offers my brother won't lift a finger. So I pull. And as I pull the knife draws another line in his palm. This new stripe grins and bleeds and changes my brother's future. It interrupts the place on his hand that once ended in crazy. My brother marvels at it.

"Now," he says, "I should try praying again. Maybe my prayers just didn't work before because I was so messed up back then."

And so my brother prays for the runaways, the bare-chested man, the lady of the headphones. Mostly though, he prays for me. He prays so hard that his hand starts to need a bandage, and the phone rings out.

"Do you feel any different yet?" he asks me.

And I want to tell him that I'm good to go, that I'll never end up like this, kneeling at a phone booth with a mind more perch than nest, my body made ready for some quiet disappearance at the hands of whoever felt like disposing of me, dirty cops, the random predators, the people who could. And I try to say that, I really do, but it doesn't come out that way in the end I guess.

"One out of two in a family isn't so bad," I say.

For people with problems, we decide, it does no good to pray. We swear never to try again. My brother's hand leaks as we swear, the line that once ended in crazy swooning beneath layers of filmy skin.

"This is temporary," he says. "I can feel it. Soon everything will grow back, scab over, heal up, and I'll be no better off than I was before."

I don't argue with him. I figure a promise might be more appropriate, and the promise proves to me that I must really love my brother, because I don't know how I could make myself do what I'm about to do otherwise. It feels good to love someone like that, to know, for once, what it's like.

"I'll find Mom," I say. "She'll have the answers."

And we shake on the promise. This at least, stops the bleeding. It keeps us warm while we wait for one more ring in the dark.

ELEVEN

Now that I know what love is, I have ideas. The first was about washing my hands. The second had something to do with that drain. The third and fourth were mistakes, they bit me, I got the hiccups. I can't remember the fifth because it had my mother in it. I think it was just like the sixth, but with more glass.

My latest idea is about a doorknob and a string. To make my teeth fly, all I have to do is smile, and tie a knot and wait for my father to open the door. He won't be home for hours. So I wait. And I try to have more ideas while I wait but there are distractions, my foot is sleeping but I can't move it and the phone is ringing but I can't answer it and the room is darkening but I can't turn on a light and then my father, he opens the door but he doesn't shut it, he just sighs and takes out a pair of scissors and cuts my mouth free.

He closes the scissors and he starts to speak because cutting always reminds him of a story he can tell, but I don't want to hear it, it's the same story I've been hearing all week.

"What do you think you're doing?" he asks, he wonders.

He believes I just want money again but I remind him that I'm not interested in anything more than enacting all the rituals I've missed, and he says that it doesn't matter how old you are—no one comes in the night to check under your pillow—and I act like I believe it because that calms him down and I let him put a pill in me because that calms him even more.

But when he's not looking I get another idea and it says I should poke around in his toolbox. Now I have that tooth surrounded. The tooth loosens itself into the sink. I think it's canine. I think it's stray. I fall asleep and leak a salty absence. And when I wake the tooth's still there, but someone must have come because there's a red map on the pillow. Its latitudes are sticky with arrows. Its avenues read the same, whichever way I turn it.

The map gives me a lot of direction. It says that if I can get into enough trouble walking like my mother did, a car will flash its lights at me and take me to see her. It doesn't say anything about my feelings, which are in my body. These days, my feelings are braining me under. I take the map with me out to the street, and I stand on the corner. There aren't too many people driving by. I put out one hip and I ask the mailman if I can do anything for him, his head turns with interest and he says yeah, if you could just step to the right and let me know if I'm about to hit that car in back of me, that would be nice.

The kid behind the movie theater is sorry, but he doesn't have any money. If he did, he says, he might take me up on it. I give him five dollars. Oh no, he says, I can't accept that, I'm the one that should be paying you. It's a loan, I say, and I get excited because there's a policeman over by the water fountain, he looks ready to catch me, even his walkie-talkie says it's over, but then the kid's friends tell him to hurry because it's about to start and he shouldn't miss the beginning, the beginning's the best part, and he leaves me, he goes up to the ticket office and says one please for a picture that makes people laugh.

The dentist tells me to open wide and swallow. I have to do what he says. I don't know how my mother did it. I wonder if she had to wear a bib too. The dentist says it won't take very long. He says it won't hurt too much. We salivate together. But I feel hopeless. Since there is no one to catch us. Not even the hygienist wants to call the police. He puts a mask on my face so he doesn't have to look at me while he finishes but when my eyes open, there's nothing on the table beside me but a wad of cotton, and I can't feel a thing.

Once again, I ready myself. My father makes his own preparations. He claims he's going out to play with his metal detector, but he wears cologne. I say I'm going to dig for clams, but I put on underwear. While I'm waiting for the bus I see him sitting in his car. I don't know whether he does this to make sure I don't follow him, or just because he likes to look at me, but once the bus pulls away I don't even wonder. I'm too busy knowing that this will be the night that I'll finally see my mother.

And I think of how I'll put her head in my lap and she'll ask if we'll always live, she'll want to know if there is no end to this. And I'll say, I never thought of that, but I guess we should decide and here's how we'll do it—if you start to bleed I'll die and if you don't I'll still die, but at least you won't need a bandage. And my mother, she'll start to bleed, she'll say she can't help it because it's been so long since she's seen me. It stabs her to know. And I'll say, it can't be like that, and I'll have to think of something, let me think, I'll say and then we'll agree that if she bleeds out of happiness I'll live always but if she seeps from some greater mourning I'll have to die because I can't keep making it so that every idea is bigger than her idea of me. My mother will laugh so hard her mouth will fill with blood. Now you've gone and done it, I'll say.

The shore's a good place to get caught. There's seaside music for sing-along bars, a carousel with its cupidity gone to rust. Now that I'm here I'm realizing she used to be here too, she could be that woman over there if that woman ever got flowers from my father that resurrected bees. She could be the lady two ladies over if that one ever raced me for a bar of soap. She could even be that girl in the dress that makes you wonder if you can see through her, the knock-kneed one with her hair fetal white, but I am acquainted with that one. Once, we were in situations together.

"Do I know you?" Tatty asks, because I'm rubbing my cheek against her shoulder. She wasn't too bad to me in the juvenile hall, but she liked to watch her hands at my throat a lot, she liked to kick me because she couldn't stub a toe on my ribs, they yielded, they let her pass, they let her know she could make her mark even as she missed it.

"Remember?" I say.

She's jabbing at a parking meter with a long stick. She has a talent for happiness, but it loves to hurt things.

"Sure," she says. "How's it going?"

Mostly, she used that talent for good, by which I mean, she started it. And then I'd hit back so she could hit again and neither of us would have to have to be free, our sentences increased, our judgments too, we were kept and final in our belonging.

I tell her I've never been better.

She gives me a smirk, the same sneaky upturn of the mouth she always gave. The smirk that says: I know I can do this, I know you'll let me get away with it. But there's something different in it now. It glares to amend her bite. Her teeth are beaded. They have traps.

"Me too," she says. "I'm getting my braces off soon. And I'm not out here for trouble. Because I've got skills now. I went back to school. I can be anything I want."

"Even a gardener?"

"Allergies," she says.

"Even a bus driver?"

"Carsick," she says.

"What about a judge?"

She pokes the parking meter, thoughtful.

"I don't think I can be a judge."

"Of course you can," I tell her. "We all can."

"Sure," she says. "Except for those losers over there. They can't make shit out of themselves." She motions to the elders brooding outside the bait shop. And she addresses their worth by halving herself; she wags her ramps and moans pelvic, her mouth snaps at the lower air.

"Maybe they don't know they're losers yet," I say. "Maybe they just need time to think."

"Forget them," she says, and she levels a fist to the parking meter. "I'm just here looking for my dog. That's the only reason I'm here. Otherwise, I'd be inside. With my dog."

"I know what you mean. I just came out here to help you find your dog too."

The streetlamps are curing our silhouettes. I can feel it. They're stretching our attachments so thin they have no choice but to rest far from our bodies.

"That's not why you're here," she says. "I know why you're here."

"That's not me anymore," I say. "I'm doing what I can. I take one pill, wash it down, I forget. Did I take that pill? So I take a pill, I wash it down—did I really take that pill?"

"I don't think you did."

"To tell you the truth," I say, "I'm just out here because I'm going to see my mom. But maybe she knows where your dog is."

Tatty smiles at me again, she gives me those glints.

"She probably stole him," she says.

"My mom didn't steal your dog. She's never stolen a dog in her life. And even if she did, she wouldn't want your dog. He won't mate near a church. He won't give a hole a bone. Your dog can't lick anyone clean."

"You haven't changed at all," she says. "Talking garbage, same as always." And she raises her fist to me, but then a car slows up by our corner so we forget about fighting because this car could mean more to our futures, and we run to sidle alongside it, we divvy up our walks to make them click into prospect and Tatty leans over and I can't really hear but I think she's asking the man inside if he's seen her dog and I guess he hasn't because he gives her money to buy a new one instead and then another car pulls up from around the corner with its lights flashing. And then I think, this is my chance, I just have to let them see me with this man who is so lonely he pays girls to turn him back into a person, and I go to put my hand on him so everyone will know there is something between us, but as my fingers reach for his shoulder I see that the shoulder

belongs to my father. He's too busy crying to even know who
I am.

My mother always knew who I was. She even wrote me
notes. There was one about being back later. It was written
on a paper cup. She'd left it on the dashboard so we'd have
water to drink and words to read in the morning. My brother
read. I did the drinking. We were in the rear seat of the car
because there was more room to stretch out there and my legs
were asleep. Or maybe they were faking sleep. I couldn't know
because we didn't have a mirror, they were all out, even the
rearviews. She'd parked us in an empty lot, just a field off the
kind of road that sees a car once in a while. My brother was
younger than me, just as he'd always been, and he spent much
of that first day rolling the window up. It took a long time to
roll that window up because the handle was stuck. But he did
it, and once it was done, finally it was night and we got out of
the car because it was easier to keep watch that way. We decided to look for crickets because they were something we could
have, and so we caught them by the shriek of their knees. We
put them in the paper cup she'd written on. We made sure they
had enough room and air. The cup sang to us for two nights. It
sang, oh no that will leave a mark.

My father's face is marked with the exact coordinates of
absolute and final sorrow, they well, they drip, they sunder
down his cheek.

"Stop crying," I say.

"It's not what you think," he tells me.

But I'm not thinking. I'm just trying to remember the last
time my hands were so together. They fit so neatly in these
holes, and they're free to do all they want, as long as I don't

have to have them in front of me.

I ask my father if there's anything he's been doing behind my back.

"I didn't think you'd understand. I didn't think you'd know that I'm just trying help people."

I explain to him that it would've been a lot more helpful if he'd just come out and told me what he wanted instead of sneaking around. I explain to him that we could've gone to see Mom together, we could've planned it right, we could've organized.

"What am I going to do now?"

I tell him that if anyone messes with him on the inside, he should just buck-fifty them.

"What's that?"

I try to explain it all: the telephone cut, the rowdy zero, the black egg tango. But it's hard to demonstrate without my hands. Instead, I work with my shoulders, my elbows. It isn't accurate, but it's the best I can do.

"That sounds like violence," he says.

He blinks, tries to speak. His voice fulfills a waver.

"Listen," he says. "It's going to be okay. I'll call the lawyer, we'll make it like this never even happened. You'll be out before you know it."

I tell him just to make sure I'm not out too fast, I don't want to go too fast, too many things have gone too fast already.

"You can visit Mom some other time. We'll make a day of it. All three of us. We'll do whatever you want."

"I want to go the aquarium."

"Of course. Yes. The aquarium."

"But the docent won't let me put my hand in the ray tank anymore."

My father promises he'll make it happen if I'll just cooperate with everyone.

I consider this. At the aquarium there are animals with longer memories. They scale and harbor and seize the littler ones
with their filigrees. The thought of it is tempting.

"But I have to see her now," I say.

He starts to cry again. He has loaded himself onto his
knees, even though the officers have said that this is not at all
necessary.

"It's all right," I tell him. "Soon, we'll all be together."

But I'm wrong because they put us in separate cars and we
drive away. We're apart, but I'm not worried. I've seen people
return before.

My mother came back skinned. A patch of hair behind her
ear was missing. She told my brother not to listen and then she
told me about the man who picked her up. He put her under
his mattress and he lay down on top of it and once in a while
he'd pull up the corner of the mattress and punch her a few
times and then he'd roll back over. I asked her if she knew
where she was. She said he just rolled back over and sometimes that was it and sometimes there was more. I asked her if
there was enough money for a hotel now, not a really nice one
or anything, just one where there was a bathtub in the room
because my brother and I were covered in bug bites and we
itched. We had sores all over ourselves, we opened them up
with our fingers and the blood ran out, but then it ran right
back in again and sealed the holes shut. She was so glad to see
us, she said.

I hope she won't mind that I haven't brought my brother.
I ask the officer if we could stop by and pick him up but I

guess she doesn't want to keep my mother waiting because she just puts her foot heavier on the pedal. I ask her to turn on the sirens because my mother likes to hear things coming, she startles easy, but that doesn't happen either, the lights sit still, and I ask Tatty if I look appropriate. I want to look appropriate for my mother. I want her to know my chest only sticks out like this because of all the breath that's there. My lungs are so bad I can't blow enough to cancel all the air I take away from everyone else.

"He comes around a lot you know," Tatty says.

I tell her that my father isn't like us. I tell her goodness attaches itself to him.

"You don't know him then. I bet I know him better than you."

I give her facts. As a kid, my father was dyslexic so he fell down a lot of wells. He won't take his shirt off in front of people. Not even to swim. His handwriting's really bad because he doesn't eat enough candy. His voice sounds younger from the hallway. He says throwing up on a boat is not something he is interested in at this time. He says it's already too late when you wake up inside a question. When I asked him what he meant by that, he just shrugged and opened up a bottle of peroxide.

"That doesn't mean anything," she says. "That means nothing. You can't know him the way I do because he tells me everything, he tells me how his wife is diseased so bad the best she can do is rot a little slower but he's never even mentioned your name."

And I think I say something back to Tatty, I think I tell her that my father knows me not by my name, but by his suffering, and I think it's her I'm talking to because I'm shouting but I could be wrong because she doesn't look at me. The officer does though. Her voice is badged and even.

"Stop asking how close we are," the officer says. "You'll be there soon enough."

At the station, I want to go to my father but he's busy getting his picture taken and the officer is wondering if I'm still a child and I figure she wants to know that because my mother's probably told them she's not so good with children, she gets children taken away from her because they need too much, they need cereal and cartoons and shoes that endure. I don't need anything, I tell the officer, I'm an adult now, and she takes my hand from where it becomes a beginning, right at the fingertip, and she blackens my index so I can leave the kind of marks that can be seen too.

And they take away my map because they're afraid I will hurt my mother if I find her. What I've done, they say, means I must be searched and they expect me to fight but I bow for them instead, I shed to prove there's nothing carried between myself and the tender separations entered by their gloves. They shine lights in me and whistle, but I am careful not to wince. Keeping quiet is harder because their pokes escort my twitch and I'm only laughing because it's so funny to be touched there. Right where the skin in my body becomes a corner. I try to stop. But that only makes me laugh more. When I come back next time, I tell them, I'll be better prepared, but I'm not sure what I say is clear because the light they're shining in my mouth is burning a hole through my head for all the laughter to leak through.

The guard doesn't know my mother. Or so her silence claims.

"Sure you do," I say. "Everyone knows her."

The guard urges me forward. She sticks her keys in my back.

"Does she know I'm coming? If she knows I'm coming—you don't have to tell me—just cough. Okay?"

The guard sighs.

"That's not the signal, but I see what you mean. Don't worry. It's all right that she knows, just as long as she doesn't know my dad's coming, at least she'll be surprised about that, right?"

The guard nods me in. Her face is something I may remember someday, if I ever care to dwell on an immovable surface.

Inside the doors there is an evening's palming, so much skin gathered it hurts to watch them become alike, at first you might think those criminals are all the same, but then I see a woman who isn't my mother and she's standing on one pink leg with the other folded to the side. And I hear someone else, she's not my mother either, she makes strange sounds and offers to braid my hair. Neither of them saw her but they'll tell me if they find anything out. And then there's Tatty, she's snarling her wired mouth into a gleam.

"Do I know you?" she says. Because I'm asking where my mother is. I want to know what they've done to her.

I smile at her. I show her my tongue, which I carry by way of identification.

"Oh yeah," she says. "That mother. She just left."

I wonder if I read that map wrong. Or maybe I wasn't as wrong as the map said I should be. I decide to make a new one, just in case.

"She heard you were coming," Tatty tells me, and she said that she might be back someday, but it'll be a very long time.

"I can wait," I tell her.

But waiting is a problem and I have nothing to attach it to. I don't know how I can continue much longer. We think on it, Tatty and I. And then she has an idea that requires me to stay still. The idea opens her knuckle. It crowns in my mouth, it cheeks an enamel noise, and then my teeth idle past and I know, finally, that I have ridded myself of all the things that have grown in my head since she left.

TWELVE

Dear Pal,

In answer to your question—sure, I could use the company, even if it is a letter from a stranger who writes to girls in jail for fun. I haven't been here for a week yet but already I could use someone to talk to. Someone who isn't the lady-friend my father brought around after he got out, after he made the people at lock-up understand that his intentions were good, that he meant no harm by asking all those flesh-sellers if they knew how he could find my mother. That he meant no harm by giving them money because he gave it to them hoping that they'd be better than my mother, that they'd take it and use it to help themselves go straight. But that's another story. My father brought that lady-friend around during visiting hours yesterday. I don't know how much he's paying her but he could do better. She just sits there in her hairdo and manicure talking a lot of questions about a huge miscarriage, a possible sentence, a reasonable plea. And I don't know where she's getting her information from but it isn't accurate. I'd never go to the warden. His office stinks of handshakes and fly traps. His face is a scabby pardon. And even if I did go to the warden I'd never say such terrible things about myself. I'd never say that I had intent. Or that I've let down my father. Or, still worse, that I've disappointed my brother. I'd never say that, just like I'd never say that I've fallen into what I've always been afraid of and that what I'm so afraid of is so real that it's making me unreal. I don't know why I would ever feel the need to confess to that.

I think I'm going to start this letter over. I'm going to write it until I get it right.

Dear Pal,

In answer to your question—no, I don't need anyone to teach me how to read in here, I've been doing it for a long time, and on my own. There are lots of other things I never got the hang of though, like swallowing a pill without tasting it or having a dream without speaking. That's why I've put in a request about the new roommate we're due to get in my cell. I asked if it would be possible to get someone nice who could teach me how to make good use of myself. I asked if it would be possible to get an older type, high as my hand here and about as heavy as a wet blanket. And it would be good if she had a nurturing aspect to her, possibly gained through a mothering background. With two kids that she hadn't seen in some time and missed badly. But when I made this request the correction officer just clicked her tongue and said that she didn't like to put relatives together in the same room. And I said what relative? I don't think she bought it though, because soon we got the new roommate and she's not who I wanted at all. She's about this tall and lifts me over her head in repetition for fun. She's an important person though, comes from a gang of people that are now out to get her. She says that if they ever find out that I was her roommate, they'll probably come and pay me a visit when I'm released. I hope they do. I expect there won't be too many people willing to be in my company when I get out.

I'm not sure if this is a good first impression for you. I can't get it right. I'm going to get it right.

Dear Pal,

In answer to your question—yes, just like on television. In the meantime I'm trying to keep myself busy, clocklike, and full of good thoughts. This is something the priest here said I could do to enumerate my soul into something higher. My soul keeps spleening into something smaller than the smallest part of me, which might be my right lung or probably my left one, whichever keeps breathing on all the things too good for me. This place isn't so bad for my development because they keep you on a schedule with the reports and the visits. Yesterday my brother came to visit me. He says that if I haven't seen our mother yet then she probably isn't here. He brought me a book to read about how meditating can make me right if I want it badly enough. He thinks he's not going to be right himself someday, but he says we just have to remember that it's not really our fault. He says it's her fault. He says that when we were spat out of our mother bits of her clung to us, her fluids, her silts, they seeped into us and our mother did a lot of drugs, which means some people would say that we did a lot of drugs, that they skulked inside us baby-wise without our knowing. But those people would be wrong.

I think we should find something else to talk about.

Dear Pal,

In answer to your question—I apologize. I know it's taking me a long time to write this. It's not that I don't want to put this letter in the mail, but that I'm afraid someone in the mailroom will read it. I don't like the idea of people around here reading my mail. I don't know why the people in the mailroom need to know our secrets. It's not like they don't have enough secrets of their own. So I just want to let you mailroom people know that if you're reading this, that's fine, that's your job, but if I see any of my secrets lying around on the floor around here, you'd better watch out. Because I'll make your eyes search for you from the floor if you do. I'll pity your minutes. I'll dress your lice. I'll give you the praise I give to germs and bug bites and bad weather. I'll phrase out your conversations until your word is just the promise of an alphabet that doesn't know your name.

Just give me one more chance, I'll get this letter right next time, I mean it.

Dear Pal,

In answer to your question—sometimes, it's okay in here, but when it's not I just make up a joke and think of the joke instead. All my jokes are in question-and-answer form, because they're funnier that way, and the funnier they are, the better they block out the bad parts. Anyhow, as I was saying, this morning I woke up feeling okay because there was a good chance I'd be able to talk to this girl Tatty who knows everything. But mostly, she just knows about how I can find my mom in such a big place. Tatty's been in solitary so I've been waiting a long time to see her. I got my pen and the back of my hand together to take some notes and I went down to Tatty's place, but when I got there it wasn't a good time for talking, because there was a guard in the cell and Tatty wasn't making any noise.

Q: How do you tell a throat from a curtain?

A: Tie it up really tight and see if it struggles.

And then the guard saw me watching so he got up and carried me by the neck back to my place, and he threw me on my bed and left. So that was okay. But the noise I made landing on my bed awoke one of my cellmates, this muscular person who was trying to nap. She doesn't like to wake up much. Unfortunately, I made that happen.

Q: What do you get when you cross a voice with a bully?

A: Same thing you get when you cross a runt with a squeal.

Then I went to see the nurse-nun around here, just because I figured she was safe to fix me, and as a nurse she might be like my dad, she might be able to make me feel like there's more to me than just this and that. And the nurse-nun told me that I just needed to negotiate with the above and see if the above would forgive me. She said that if I was forgiven I would feel it in my heart.

Q: How did the prayer make ends meet?

A: That sounds like a nice idea.

Q: Why did the psalm hold its breath?

A: Because its hiccup was a plea that went nowhere.

Q: How do you help people discover their cruelty?

A: With a knife, but they'll find it on their own eventually.

Q: How does a six-month sentence make it through the night?

A: We'll see.

Dear Pal,

In answer to your question—I'm not sure what you mean by that because I can't read your letter in the dark. If you see my mother please tell her that I

THIRTEEN

We know that the world must have a lot of people in it if it can afford to keep so many of us locked up. On the inside, we wait to be good enough to join them someday. To become good enough we have to walk back and forth, back and forth up the long hall. We have to sew jeans, share smokes, see others do as they'd like with us. We have to forgo and go on, somehow on, anyhow on. We have to mark lines on the walls to indicate the passage of days, and then, when the marks become too many for us to look at, we have to erase them. The dust from the erasure of the days is powerful stuff. I've collected a small store in my pocket that I inhale on lonely nights. It takes effect quickly and makes my brain mind itself, but it doesn't put my sleeplessness to rest. Still, not sleeping through the night isn't so bad because it lets me think more about my mother.

She must be here somewhere. Even Tatty says so. I get her to talk with me in the laundry room. This costs me two weeks of washing her clothes and kissing her hand. I apply my lips accordingly.

"That'll do," she says, and she pulls away from me. I can tell that lately, something's been getting under her skin.

"Is that a new tattoo?"

"You like it?"

"I might've gone a little darker round the tail but that's a nice kite."

"Yeah. I should get it touched up, but the best have all been paroled lately. There's nobody good left, nobody with any real talent."

"I can do tears really well. I can do them for free."

"I'm not interested in your tears."

"I can learn quick. Anything you want."

"What about roses?"

"No," I admit. "No roses."

"Daggers then? Koi? Diamonds? Ribbons? Birds?"

"I do birds."

"What kinds of birds?"

"Mocking. Love. Blue."

"Can I see a sample?"

I pull up my pant leg and show her my ankle.

"That's a scab," she says.

"If you say so."

"I don't understand why people say you're so smart."

"I'm not, you know," I tell her. And then I tell myself too. It does my soul good to hear it. Sometimes my soul forgets how hard life is because we spend so little time together. It makes itself scarce because of my brain. The two of them don't get along so well. They don't have much in common, I guess. Except for the quarters they share with my diseases, a scrawny nature overgrown with the wages of failure—

"What are you talking about?" Tatty asks.

I beg her pardon. I didn't know that she could hear me, I

explain.

"Is that all you wanted to say to me?"

I tell her that what I really wanted to say is to ask her if she knows anything about where my mother might be. That's all.

"How should I know?"

I tell her she should know because she knows everything else that I don't, usually.

"I don't know where your mother is. But I know someone who might."

"Who?"

"If I tell you, you have to compensate for the information."

"Anything. I'll do anything."

"Mrs. Ollie," she says. "Go ask Mrs. Ollie."

"Who's that?"

Tatty is patient with my ignorance. She explains it all to me: Mrs. Ollie is the sweetest of us, the oldest, the most prophetic. She's been given the power to know everything because she was pulled from a dead woman at birth. It was compensation for having to crawl from a cold hole at such a young age. Tatty reminds me that I know a thing or two about compensation.

"What do I have to do for you in return?" I ask.

"When you see that crazy Ollie," she says, she smiles. "Be sure to hurt her for me."

Mrs. Ollie draws her knife and fork alone. People don't like to sit with her because she's seized by hiccups whenever she's busy knowing the affairs of the world. At least, that's what people say, but really, she just makes them uncomfortable by being too aged. She's proof that ears dull and eyes see better days, that the body grows old but the body never grows too old for jail. I cross the room to her bench and a din goes up from the hall to accompany me; the diners bang tray to table, the servers clap their spoonfuls, the lunch line stomachs howl. When I sit by her she hands me her fork and knife, expectant, so I cut her loafy meats for her, organize her gravies, butter up. I try not to look at her. She doesn't have to try not to look at me. She's a proper old yardbirder, hair beneath a scarf, napkin at her throat. She folds her hands to connect their spots. She prays:

"Oh Heaven, oh Not-I, oh Above-Me, this food is bad, but I'm sure it will bless my body, and the day has been too hot but I guess it's almost over and there's this mental cripple sitting next to me but I guess thy will be done and it's going to be a long night but I guess that will give me more time to think about the wrongs I did, like not double-checking that recipe because I thought it was a good recipe and I never thought it would turn out like that, all that fire, all that smoke, the police-man saying that I was a poor sort of chef, engaging in some dirty cookery, some bad druggery, the kind of stimulation that's too dangerous for an old citizen like me and too illegal besides. Amen."

Mrs. Ollie looks up from her prayer. She sees me eating without praying and swallowing without ceasing. She prongs me with her fork.

"I don't know how," I say.

She instructs me to express my thanks and ask for blessings. Like a conversation. But with a face too large to be thought. Like a letter. But with handwriting too small to be read.

I pray:

"Thanks for putting me here so I can find my mother. And so I can have some time to think about the all wrongs I've done and all the wrongs I've always wanted to do, like breathe on a church window in winter so I can draw a name in vain on the breath-patch or beat my fifth foster father with a rolling pin till he truced. I'd like to recess kids who eat for fun, make them take back the laughs they laughed in earshot of my empty stomach—"

Mrs. Ollie interrupts, she puts a hand on mine and squeezes.

"How'd I do?"

"I wouldn't know," she says, "if you're capable of anything better."

She doesn't seem to like me much. So I give her an offering, sacrifice my meal tray to her. It's not much of a sacrifice, but it feels good to see bread multiply by the crumb and collect in her jaw, even if most of it just falls out of her mouth and back onto my plate.

"I hear that you have all the information," I say.

"That's right. What kind of information do you need?"

"There are a lot of things I'd like to know, but mostly—"

"Wait," she says. "Don't tell me."

And she thumps a fist on the table for emphasis as the rest of the diners scatter.

"You want to know how your parole will go? You want to know if they have any sympathy for a woman who exploded her house in a culinary fit and made the woods reek for days of a most profitable medicine?"

"Not really—"

"You want to know what your big mistake was? Did you just overheat the reaction or were the chemicals all wrong?"

"That's not—"

She claps a hand over my mouth and pauses thoughtfully.

"Don't tell me. It's your cellmates isn't it? You're interested in how they're planning on jumping you because they don't like the way you know too much?"

"My cellmates are going to jump me?"

She nods.

"But I'm going to overpower them right? I'm going to shuck their noses with the back of my hand and tell them they should be ashamed of themselves for letting their noses bleed like that all over the floor. And I'm going to make them take off their shirts and lay those shirts over those nosebleed puddles so I don't have to bloody my feet while I smoke their cigarettes, one by one, stick by stick, puff by drag by ring by blow. Right?"

She shakes her head.

"But I'm going to be okay right? I'm going to rise up. Or roll over. Or protect my chest because my face can take it. I'm going to charm my way into mercy, right? And they'll promise that it'll never happen again, right?"

Mrs. Ollie points to her throat. I'm not sure if that means the same thing as shaking your head or not, but pretty soon I don't have much time to figure anything out at all because she's choking, her mouth gaped so wide I can see a silver filling for every time someone's died on me. And I'm not going to let this one die on me. At least not until I find out where my mother is. So I pound on her chest to thwack the obstructions out of her. She blushes red. I put my hands around her throat and squeeze. She blooms white. I ask her if she knows where my mother is. A rasp leaks from her throat in answer because her insides aren't cooperating. I squeeze her harder. She points a finger at a corrections officer. The corrections officer must know where my mother is. The officer hustles towards us. Then his hands are on me. My hands are on Mrs. Ollie, and they have a fair handle on her fit. But the officer is hauling me off, she makes me let go, and as I'm dragged away I see Mrs. Ollie cough up what was harming her. The eaters in the dining hall cheer and congratulate the cause of this breathlessness as it lies there on the floor. It's just a scrap of meat. I can see where it's coming from, lying there like that. Both of us are licked.

Even in solitary I have company. There's this officer who's helping me get used to my surroundings, he's a skinny mite with a blunt stick at his side for company. I've seen him around before, buffing that stick to a shine on the cloth that covers the backs of inmates. I've tried to keep my distance from him.

I tell the officer I need some time to myself.

"I have to be here," he says, and he holds up this new outfit I have to wear. "I'm supposed to make sure you don't kill yourself in here."

I wonder aloud why I would kill myself now. At least that's what I think I wondered. When the officer answers me, he makes it sound like I was wondering about something else.

"What do you mean how?" he says. "There's plenty of methods. I mean, if you really want to do something, there's always a way."

And he makes a lot of demonstrations with his hand and the toilet and recommends implements that he can smuggle in for me at a decent price.

"But don't kill yourself," he adds. "That would look bad."

Then he goes very quiet and picks up one of my hands. He touches my fingerprints and his mouth falls open a little, he breathes a little harder.

"Why did you want to hurt Mrs. Ollie?"

I tell him I was only—

He wants to know if I have something against people, because he could understand that he says, it seems reasonable to him.

I try to explain—

"Take off your clothes. We've got to change you."

And so I try to coax my zipper to part, but my zipper won't be moved. It brags steely teeth, casts dental glances up at my empty jaw. I think it thinks it's better than me.

"This zipper is stuck up," I say.

"You're moving it the wrong way. You're supposed to move it down," the officer says, and then he demonstrates on himself.

"Like so," he says. I try to do it in time with him, but no budge.

"Sometimes you have to wiggle it a little," he says. "Like so." He applies his fingers again, but my pants remain un-latched. And then there's a catch. The catch happens against my skin. A welt broods against my stomach. I try to pull my pants off but I go unsteady instead.

"One leg at a time," the officer advises. "Let's try the right first."

When my legs are free the officer tries to pull a nightgown over my eyes, but I won't let him.

"I can dress myself," I say. But this isn't altogether true. First my mother dressed me. I believe it was for a picnic at the park. I was bootied, bibbed, ruffled, wore a pacifier in my mouth and a pin in my pants. In the care of fosters I was draped by a procession of fingers I don't care to remember, I was hand-me-down and low-about-the-hem. In the hospi-tal my best nurse dressed me. She made sure my bandages matched, that my shirtfront was free of pill-crumbs. At my grandparents' bedside Babcia snapped me into a series of pajamas that kept me from touching myself, zippered affairs with feet attached. They rubbed me the wrong way. My father couldn't bear to look. He dressed me with his eyes closed. I was striped on plaid and stained all over. In lockup, I can't find anyone to help me on a regular basis so I settle for whoever is passing by and give them favors to hook me up garment-wise. I make their beds so my buttonhole might be closed, shine their shanks for the sake of my shoelaces. Most times, I'm presentable. I wear a pill in my cheek, a book beneath my arm. Now, with no one to help me I must be looking bad. Something's not right, I can feel it.

"You've got the wrong hole," the officer says.

"I'm not sure how I got this way."

"Use your head," he recommends.

But that isn't so easy for me to do, because from the opening in the garment where my face should hang, my arm dangles instead.

I ask the officer to help me. I tell him I'll do anything just to get things right.

"Can you get me another job?"

"This job doesn't seem so bad."

"Can you make my daughter talk to me again?"

"Daughters have their reasons."

"Can you make her just accept my apology at least?"

"I'm sorry."

"I thought so," he says, and he leaves me there, rearranged, my parts pieced out into uselessness. My arm is a poor substitute for a head since it has no brains. It culminates in a wrist that can't do my breathing for me, and a palm that can't talk or chew. While it sits solidly on my side, my head is no better. My head can't hold things the way my arm can. It can't even tell me how to get out of a situation with a hole. In these circumstances, I decide the most sensible thing to do is to bang my head against the wall. My arm decides it. We figure that if maybe we make enough noise my mother will hear us. She'll know it's us by the thud on the wall, the clap of my scalp. She'd know that sound anywhere. And she'll come to me, she'll put my body to rights.

I pound my head on the wall. Two knocks answer it back. It must be my mother. I knew she was near. I pound twice more. My skull beats out a sorry code.

The door unlocks. The officer steps in, swings his keys.

"You're not my mother," I point out.

"No more of that bang-bang, okay?"

"I might be able to stop if I could see my mother."

"I don't know where your mother is, but if you keep that up I'm going to have to take you to where there's a lot of padding and not much room to move."

"Is that where my mother is? Somewhere with a lot of padding?"

"I wouldn't be surprised," the officer says.

So I clap my head on the cement once more. My brain pangs in on this applause, it fists itself before bowing, pulls a heavy curtain, and I see a thought encore into grey, encore into black and I can't help but think that if I could apprehend the thought that makes me insist on living, then I wouldn't have to do such a bang-up job at having a fighting chance. I could curl and be finished. But the thought of ending it all just slips past me once more. It finds a new hideout where the stakes have been raised into a lump on my forehead, a swollen temple that charms me to sleep.

When I wake there are stitches complicating my forehead. The girl in the bed next to me points them out from behind an excess of belly, a sweaty fertility hovered over by a doctor with an instrument that amplifies its mutters. The belly bucks and intones a plea. But the girl doesn't pay any attention. She has eyes only for my forehead.

"That'll leave a mark," she says.

I tell her that no one asked her, and even if they did ask her it certainly wasn't me.

"Don't call yourself no one," she says. And this is when I recognize her by the sorority of burns on the back of her hand. They mean that she belongs to the Pockets. The Pockets are full of themselves. They have their reasons. The Pockets are the biggest girl gang going around here, bigger than the Clocks, stronger than the Plagues, smarter than the Filigrees. They organize the common cold, have dibs on the phones, final say on the dinner menu. If you're not a Pocket you don't see meat. They run the seeing-eye dog program. If you're not a Pocket you don't get to pet. They rig the talent show. If you're not a Pocket it's best not to tap dance. Or speak. Or look. If you're not a Pocket it's best to fold into yourself and hold nothing, because they'll be sure to take it from you as they walk by.

I tell the Pocket that I need some space.

"Everyone knows about you," she says.

"You mean—that incident with the bone? That wish was the bone's idea. It wasn't mine."

"Not that one," she says. "That one's new to me."

"You mean about how my teeth left me? They know about that?"

"Anyone can see that," she snorts.

"What then?"

She says that everyone on the inside—the old-timers, the good-behavers, the three-strikers, the usual suspects, the final-appealers—they know too. They know where I'm coming from. They know whose daughter I am. They know she wasn't a terrible person, even if she might've been a little too bad for her own good.

"You know about my mother?"

The Pocket nods. Her belly nods with her.

"Where is she?"

The girl tells me that my mother's on the outside but she's not sure where. The outsiders—the guards, the janitors, the nurses, the warden, the priests, the nuns, the protesters, the visitors, the pen pals—they might know too, which means the girl herself might know someday, because she's going to be out there soon enough.

"You?"

"Sure," she says. "I'm going to have myself a little vacation."

"Really? For how long?"

"Just a few days or so, maybe a week if I'm lucky. In the hospital, they'll give me ice cream and maybe even take the cuffs off if the baby's cute enough. They always like watching a mother hold a cute baby. If the baby's ugly, then I don't know. They might not let me spend much time with it then. But even then I'll have the drive home to look forward to. And if there's any window I'll probably get to see different trees than we have here. Maybe even some different birds."

And then the Pocket starts to fill with tears. I can tell what she's thinking just from the way she surveys her stomach.

"Your baby won't be ugly," I tell her. "You'll probably get to hold it for a long time before they take it away."

"You think so?"

"You'll probably even have enough time to sing it a song. You have a song picked out yet?"

"No. You ever have a baby? You know what kind of songs they like?"

I consider this for a moment. I haven't had a baby before but I had something close. Once, I had a growth. Just an infectious

little virus on the lining of me. The doctors called it dangerous and they took it from me. I couldn't help but feel empty
afterwards. I never got to hold it or even see what it looked
like. Sometimes, when I feel particularly sad, I write a song for
the growth, in my head, about leaving well enough alone. But I
don't tell any of this to the girl.

"I've heard they don't really like songs anyway," I say.

She nods, and drums a hopeful rhythm on her distention,
right above where the button's popped, blooming like some
puffy sea creature on the veined stretch.

"My mother could help me with your baby if you could
find her," I say. "She worked with me when I was a baby. My
brother too. We turned out all right."

"I don't know where your mother is."

"But I know you know someone who does."

"Ask Minus," the girl says. "She's our leader now. She
knows."

I point out the obvious problem with this. No one is al-
lowed to speak to Minus until they become a Pocket and to
become a Pocket a person has to pass a lot of tests. I don't
have any answers, or at least, I don't have the answers people
like to hear.

The girl draws a deep breath, and then another, and another, and then she clutches her belly. It's obvious. That she's
giving something a lot of thought.

"I'll give you answers," she offers.

"Will you?"

"But don't tell anyone. I could get into trouble."

"I won't."

"First thing you need to know—"

"Wait. I need to write this down."

The girl hands me the pen from behind her ear.

"You need to know," she says, "if you have a body you can do anything and if you have a body anything can be done to you. That's how it works."

"That's one of the answers?"

"Just some advice. Thought you could use it."

I figure she might have a point and so I write it down on the back of my hand.

"Now what?" I ask.

"I wish it was over already," the girl says, and she bites her lip.

"That's it?" I say. "That's the big answer?"

I would've thought they'd have something better than that, but I write it down anyway.

"No," the girl says. "I mean, this is it."

A doctor comes between us before she can give me more answers to keep on hand. He blocks my view of everything but her legs, they're spending a lot of distance apart, and he prepares a needle to shoot in her vein. I look away. I can't look. And then I look through the blanks between the fingers I've got over my face, because I know just how many accidents can fit on the tip of the needle. I watch it dive into her arm. It burrows into the vein and the girl's face goes slack and I can tell by how quickly they wheel her away that everything may not be going well, but that soon, not long from now, it will be over.

FOURTEEN

I know the words on my hand stand for something, but they don't sit well with my skin. Once, the words answered to me, they were sure and steady in their script, printed reminders of what I have to do; now that I'm out of the infirmary they just shrug in outline, fade further, surrender ink. I'll have to find new answers as I go along so as not to waste too much time. I've got a lot of Pockets to go through in order to find my mother. Three, to be exact.

The first Pocket is busy at her post, disciplining her pet. I've seen her around before, flipping her braid and dragging that dictionary around on a dirty old leash. She makes that book beg for table scraps, kicks it when it doesn't come, yells when it won't fetch her slippers. Together, they share a strained relationship, one preoccupied with the custody of certain adjectives.

"I own you," she's telling her pet. "And don't you forget it. I'm smarter than you, and I know what's best."

She strokes the dictionary's yellow spine and coos, splits it open, begins to read. When I clear my throat she peers over the index, a person little more than two eyes and a paper cut.

"I have business with Minus," I tell her.

"What sent you?"

I could tell her the truth, which is that I'm not quite sure, but instead, I go with the less obvious answer. I tell her I'm my mother's daughter and that my mother was like her. She was one of them. Which means that I'm half one of them too.

"Not quite. You'll have to pass our tests first. We can't just let anyone be a Pocket. We've got standards. I have to ask you some questions, just to see how you'd handle life as one of us."

"I'm ready," I say. I put my hand on her dictionary in the interest of maintaining the honesty of my answers.

"If you were a Pocket," she asks, "when would you strike a match?"

"Only when it becomes violent. And all the other times in between."

"Good. And who does it hurt more?"

"What?"

"Just out of curiosity—who does it hurt more? You or the match?"

"Oh. The match I think."

"Is that your answer?"

"It could hurt me too. But I've caught fire before. I'm still here. The match wouldn't be."

"Right. Now, Pockets usually share everything. But what's the one thing we'd like you to keep to yourself around here?"

"Is it that thought I keep thinking about how I'll never be able to look at both my eyes in the palm of my hand?"

"Actually, the standard answer is 'disease.' But we wouldn't want that thing you're talking about either. You're good. I'm going to have to make these harder. Next question."

"Is this the last one?"

"What if it is? Will you be sad to have to move on, to have to leave me behind? When you and I were only just getting to know each other?"

"I'll regret it," I say.

"What's that supposed to mean?" she asks, and at first I think that I've offended her but then I see that she's turning pages, she's turning them to the *r*'s, and then her eye settles on a meaning that makes her mumble wearily. She takes out a pen, circles the definition and dashes off some stars, a wake of five-armed harpies that make their point around the page. Then she shuts the book and resumes the interrogation.

"Last question," she says, and she hugs the dictionary to her chest. "Was that person who swore they'd tell the truth really lying to you?"

"I know this one. I think it sounds familiar. Did the person lie to me or my brother?"

"No hints."

So I think back, back to when my mother said that to me, that time down at the bridge with a rooster crowing nearby. My mother, she said, everything I tell you is true, pretty, solid, warm, and then I up and sneezed. And that's when she said the most important thing of all. That's when she blessed me.

I decide I'm going to go with the safest answer.

"She was lying."

"True," the Pocket says. "Though she might've meant well, don't you think?"

This is one question she doesn't wait for me to answer, she just nods me along, and I thank her, I tell her that it's been a pleasure, the way I've heard my father say to people he doesn't know what to do with, and she asks me if I can repeat that word again, so I do. It's a pleasure, I tell her, and then I go to shake her hand goodbye but she's too busy leafing through her pet, making her way past the *n*'s and the *o*'s, past "parable," past "punish."

"That's taking it too far," I tell her, and I guide her back to the right page, towards a synonym for happiness and contentment, before I move on.

The second Pocket is a muscle-bound ancient in a pair of bunny slippers. She's tendoned all over, and both her arms swarm with silver hair, but I'm guessing one is better behaved than the other, because one wrist is braceleted to the silver bars. It looks like she's been there so long that she's had no choice but to become silver too. While her gleam is intimidating, she seems peaceable enough as she tends her garden, which is less a garden than a flowerpot full of bobby pins. She sticks the pins in a row, but isn't happy with the arrangement. She furrows the dirt and plants them instead. Then she spits in the pot and turns to me.

"This is a test of strength," she says, and she offers me her free hand. I don't know where that hand has been but it's stickier than mine ever was, and has smells in variety. It smells of barbells and finger traps. It smells of soap if soap is made of curses that have been rolled in black snow and dried by the light of a rosary bead. But I know what I have to do. I breathe deep and lower myself.

"That's uncalled for," she says. And she sits on the floor and rolls up her sleeve so her free arm can challenge me to a wrestle. We put our hands together and make conversation.

"So you're her kid are you?"

"Mostly," I say.

I floor her knuckles.

"We'll go two out of three," I say.

She shrugs and readies her arm for another round.

"Did my mom ever talk about me?" I ask.

"Once in a while. Usually when people were listening."

"I hope they were always listening."

"Usually," she says. "They were."

And then I lay her arm to rest once again. It goes down without the slightest fight.

"You aren't even trying," I point out.

"I am," she argues. "You're just strong. You win. Go on. Get on your way."

I don't believe her and I tell her so.

"Why do you have to make everything so hard for yourself?" she asks.

"Just one more time," I beg.

She shakes her head and starts to turn her attention to her garden.

"We're done here," she says, and then her silver arm tries to wave me away. It flutters in the air. I seize it just so I can be sure that I'm able. I level it and get on a bended knee. I hear the arm crack beneath the weight of me.

"Are you happy now?" she cries.

I tell her that it depends.

"On what?"

"Is my happiness part of the test? Do I have to be happy in order to continue?"

"No."

I tell her that's a relief because I don't get too happy about hurting people, but she refuses to look at me, she just tests the joints of her arm, and I start to leave, but not without taking out this safety pin that holds one of my shirt buttons on first. This second Pocket won't accept my gift though.

"Those kinds don't grow into keys," she explains, and I apologize for my ignorance before leaving her alone to water the brass.

Midair, the ticks somersault, the lipstick arcs, the mirror turns. They halo above the head of the juggler, this final Pocket whose hands are outnumbered by all that she can't carry. Even though her hands are full, I wish I had something to give her. Maybe she'd be friendlier that way, but for now I'll just have to respect her sour distance. She bites a blue-red lip in concentration, scoffs at the stitches in my forehead, and doesn't so much speak as spit in my direction.

"Here's the deal," she says. "If you can tell me what I'm thinking I'll let you through."

She skips a beat while juggling and one of the ticks, a comely little ball of blood, falls from above and lands at my collar. I feel his tidy burrow.

"Deal," I say. "Starting now?"

"Yes. Now."

"Right now? Because your thoughts might move really quickly. I wouldn't want to tell you what you're thinking two thoughts after you already thought it."

"Go."

"I can't. You better give me a signal."

"Like this?" she asks.

"Yes, like that. But maybe—with a different finger."

"Go. Already. Now."

"You're thinking now—you're having a thought—is it about girls in leotards making sandwiches in the desert?"

"I'm afraid not," she says, and juggles faster.

"Is it about two-faced bacteria?"

"Not quite."

"Forked sticks?"

"Sorry."

"Rope burn?"

"I've got to be going," she says, and she rises from her chair.

"Guts full of shiners?" I say. "Flaccid little pearls of vengeance? Mature oceans? A no-brainer set somewhere near the end of the world where the libraries are sopping and there's a dirty word carved onto the fencepost?"

"That's eight," she says. "You've got two left."

"Did I mention rope burn?"

"One more," she says, and she holds that finger up again so I can count on its bitten nail. I should have known better, earlier. Her insides aren't so hard to guess. She's not too different from me, or anyone else on the inside for that matter.

"You're starting to think you don't belong here," I say.

She drops everything she's kept up in the air, the ticks, the mirror, the lipstick.

"That kind of thinking will get you places," she says, and then she grasps me by the chin and initiates my mouth with paint. "Now would you like to have a look at yourself?"

I decline. She knows why.

"Don't worry," she says. "You won't have to look at yourself because you're not yourself. You're one of us now."

She's right. But I don't need to look to know. I can feel it. My face is farced with dents and dimpled into a pleasant fakery, its cheeks ruptured with a countenance I've not felt much since being here, an attack of expression that mugs its way toward something bright.

"Keep smiling," she advises.

I let my gums squat in full view so that between me and the world there's just a crescent of emptied stumps.

"Maybe you shouldn't smile quite so much," she says, and she leads me into the quarters of Minus.

The other girls in the room can't stop smiling either. They're so happy to get to touch the bullet. I don't understand the point in it. It's just a shell of a thing, a pellet shot with a silencer. Still, that bullet knows how to draw a following. There's so many of us here that I can't make out where one girl ends and another begins. Their bodies overlap and amputate each other as they clamor their hands forth to bring offerings to the bullet. They bring cigarettes and laundry soap and postage stamps. They bring travel magazines and teabags and dollar bills that fold around fingers wedding-style.

I ask the final Pocket what's so great about this bullet. I can't understand why everyone thinks it's so special. It's not like there aren't a whole lot of other bullets in the world. And it's not like it can hurt people any worse than I could, if it came down to it.

"You're just jealous."

I don't admit that she's right. I just let her lean into me to whisper the revelation.

"That bullet is a miracle," she says.

"I've never heard of anything good coming from a bullet."

"Tell that to the women who get paroled," she argues.

"I can't," I say. "I'm in here."

"Well there you go," she says, and I could admit that she has a point but I don't have a chance to because she's already telling me the history of the bullet.

The bullet lives in Minus's spine. It ventured out of its chamber one evening to case her joints before settling on the small of her back. It's been with her longer than her hips and even some of her teeth. She grew up around it. They never caught the father who did it to her because he was busy putting other bullets in his family and then a final one in his brain. Some people say that the bullet makes Minus special but really, this is just another way of saying that Minus can't walk. She lives on the shoulders of Gloria.

"Who's Gloria?"

"When you see Minus, you see Gloria too," the juggler says, and she pushes me forward. She tells me to introduce myself and instructs me not to stare at the girl above, or the girl below, because both are equally vulnerable, despite their joint efforts to stand strong and straight.

"I'm not sure what I can say about myself," I say, and then if I'm still speaking I don't know what I'm saying because I'm too busy taking in the person or people in front of me. Or at least, what I can see of them, since most of Gloria's face—and the patchy burns it bears—is obscured by the fall of hair from Minus's scalp. Together they have one body with two mouths and four breasts and just as many arms. Plus, a slouch. It seems like a well-balanced partnership, with the only important difference between the two being cigarettes and gum. On high, there's bubbles and a broken spine, and below, there's smoke and scars, but their mouths seem to have the same ideas, even if Minus does all the talking. She asks me who I am, and I try to give her a fair indication of where I'm coming from but apparently my answer isn't good enough.

"I don't speak shrug," she spits.

Gloria orders everyone to leave with a wave of her scorched hand and the women file away to await another chance for worship, they stuff their offerings in their clothes and mumble out, a disappointed congregation. I'm sad to see them go. I don't like being alone much. The double company of Minus and Gloria would seem to be a cure for that, but looking at them only makes me feel lonelier, because they've got such a good deal going, so many arms and legs at their disposal, each multiplying the possibilities of physical affection. I'd like a set-up like that myself someday, and my longing must be obvious because Minus looks down at me curiously from her great height, a height proportionate to the size of her question.

"What do you really want?" she asks.

It's difficult to look in their quartet of eyes like this, but I've heard that making eye contact is important while you speak because people won't trust you otherwise. So I take turns looking at them. First I look at Gloria, I try to put her at ease by pointing out the disfigurement of my own forehead, but she still doesn't want to be seen. She retreats behind the hair curtain, singes it on her cigarette. So I look at Minus instead.

"I hear you have a bullet in your possession."

"Yeah," she says. "My boyfriend said I could keep it."

"I thought it was your dad."

"Dad, boyfriend, you know how it goes."

"Sure," I say, even though I'm not sure I do.

"So why would the bullet want to help you?" Minus asks.

"Because I'm my mother's daughter?"

Minus looks down at Gloria and they have a furtive discussion via the whites of their eyes before our conversation is resumed.

"We heard that when your mother called you didn't come to see her. Is this true?"

"Who did you hear that from? Because whoever said that is lying."

"The bullet told us so."

"Oh."

"Are you calling the bullet a liar?"

"Not really."

"And have you brought anything for the bullet?"

"Yes, Mi—"

"You may call us your tallness," Minus says, and then she gets this look, they both do. They look at me like they can't see me, even with all those eyes, and it's like their thoughts are wherever thoughts go to forget themselves. Their stares continue like a contest till I cough to remind them that they're not alone, and their heads nod to attention.

"What were we saying just now?"

"You were saying that I could address you as my tallness?"

"No. After that."

"You were wondering if I've brought anything for the bullet?"

"That's it."

"I brought sugar," I say. "Your tallness."

I drop the pink envelope into an outstretched hand, courtesy of Gloria. She holds it up to the lamp so light can steal through the sweetness. It casts a square and lonesome shadow at my feet.

"What's a bullet supposed to do with a pile of sugar?"

I try to think of an answer. I consider the needs of the modern bullet, its whims, its angles. But before I can say anything that glaze slips over their faces for a moment, and then they rouse with a jerk.

"What were we saying this time?" Minus asks.

"First, you were thanking me for the sugar. And then you were wondering what you could do to help me find my mother."

"You can call us your loftiness. And we'd like to help you. The problem is that we gave your mom three quarters to make that call. And then those quarters went to waste. You wasted them."

"My loftiness," I say. "I'm sorry."

"You know what we could've used those three quarters for?"

"Not much?"

"Maybe not a lot to you," Minus says. "You can walk and all. But I can't walk. So quarters mean a lot to me. You know what happened to us because we were short two quarters?"

"I can imagine," I say.

"We had to—what did we have to do again?" Minus asks. She whispers into Gloria's ear and Gloria just shakes her head behind the shelter of her other half's hair.

"Apparently, we can't remember what happened to us," Minus concludes. "But I'm sure we could've done without it."

"Did it happen to both of you?"

They nod their heads together in a bevy of unisons.

"And you can't recall anything? Not even between the two of you?"

"I think it's coming back to me," says Minus. "Yes, I remember something. It has a light bulb in it. And a window."

She lowers her ear to Gloria, deftly flipping the lobe aside so as not to burn herself on the immovable cigarette.

"And Gloria remembers something about laughing," she reports.

"Who was doing the laughing?"

"That's the problem, even between the two of us, we can't remember anything. There's too much for us to think about from minute to minute. It's too much for us. We're not enough for it. We have other things to worry about. Like how we're going to walk from here to there. It takes up all our time. We don't have enough time to think about remembering what came before this. We have years and years between us in lock-up but we can't waste them remembering. We figure we'll remember when we finally get out of here. We'll probably have forgotten everything entirely by then."

This is when I make my best offer.

"I'll do the remembering for you," I say. "I'll write it all down for you. I'll remember so you don't have to."

"No," she says. "That's too much to ask of anyone. Thanks. But no."

"I'd do a good job," I say. "I'll do the best I can. I won't leave anything out. I'll make the good things bigger and the bad things true enough."

Minus blinks.

"What were we saying again?"

I consider my reply before speaking. But not for long. It doesn't take long to realize that a lie is the best thing for all of us right now.

"You were asking me to make it mean something. You said you want it to mean something, in the end."

"Was Gloria in agreement with me?"

"Yes."

"Oh," she says. "I remember now." And she seems to enjoy remembering. I have to remind her that I'm here for other reasons too. I'm here to find out where my mother is. I'm here to find out how to find her. I need to know if I can be helped.

"It's not up to us," Minus says. "It's up to the bullet. Listen to the bullet."

Really, it's just a shell of a thing, that oracle, but it's out of my reach. I have to pull up a chair to stand on and then I put my ear to where the bullet once entered.

"I don't hear anything," I say.

"You have to listen. Very closely."

The bullet has a squeak of the highest caliber. It says that I shouldn't mind Gloria. It says that it's not easy, the life of a cripple. It coughs a bit. It asks me if I'm still there.

"I'm listening."

The bullet tells me that tomorrow morning there will be an indoor problem, a ruse on the blocks, a din in the hall, and during this distraction I should lift a few tiles beneath the sink of Minus-Gloria's cell and lower myself down into a hole. And I should be on the lookout as I go. Because when I hit bottom there'll be a note with my mother's whereabouts on it—

"Where is she?"

The bullet sighs. It tells me that my mother is now in the employ of a theatre just outside of city limits, some wreck of a place that no one should be going to. But since I have to go there, I should crawl through the tunnel and take care not to lose my stitches in it. It'll be a long shot to the end, the bullet tells me, but when I get that far I'll see a corner turning, and then I should hoist myself up into the outer mantle of the world and look both ways before I leave. It's that easy, the bullet claims. And I can figure it out from there, right? I'm a grown girl or at least a girl, right? That's what the bullet says, and I'm so happy that a bullet would think so kindly of me that I lift my ear from its entrance before it's even finished speaking. I want to tell my friends the good news, but before I have a chance to say anything, a cigarette falls on my shoe. It carries its ashes tidy and I can still hear the words of the bullet as I stoop to pick it up. But when I go to restore the cigarette to the mouth of Gloria I find that returning it won't be so simple. Her lips are too busy moving. When she sees me looking she stops, and the voice of the bullet stops too.

FIFTEEN

So it's like this in the end, a hole less a hole than just another opening for my head to come through. My head comes first. Then my shoulders. It's snowing out. I look both ways before leaving the hole but I don't look back, because too much snow has passed and I've torn the stitches from my forehead because the wound on it claims that there's no such thing as closure. I don't think the bus driver agrees. She stares down my wound while I pay the fare in ice. She tells me that this isn't an ambulance, this isn't my ride, this bus doesn't stop at the hospital. I tell her that it's okay, I tell her that part comes later, and I sit down next to a woman who holds her children tighter at the sight of my face. I like the fact that I have that effect on people. If there's anything good about me, I think, there's that. I make them hold their children tighter. Because of me, I think, parents guard infantile joints and minute spleens and cranial plates that take their own sweet time to fuse—

The woman taps my shoulder and then wipes her tapping finger clean on a square of tissue. After getting my attention, she pulls her boys, preciously groomed youngsters with inspirational lunchboxes, close to her immovable bosom.

"Do you have to be so loud when you talk to yourself?" she wonders. "I don't want to be rude, but if you're the speaker and the listener, can't you know what you're talking about without yelling?"

I tell the woman that she has a point. But it's not one that I can pay much attention to at the moment because my voice is kind of drowning it out.

"Doesn't seem like you have much nice to yell about. Why do you bother talking to yourself at all?" She covers her boys' ears so they're spared from my reasoning, or at least, from the sound of it, which I'll admit isn't the best it could be, since my stutter seems to have caught a cold. So I make my explanation soft.

I tell the lady that I was only talking to myself, because talking to myself is the closest I can get to being with people I can't talk to. She stares at me, confused, before swaddling her family in her arms and staking out a different seat, one that distances itself from my voice while offering the privilege of a window.

The lady probably just wanted a better perspective on things. I'd share my own, but I can't spare much of it, because I need some help to see that the nests out there are only empty because they want to be, and those snowballs don't have chances because they prefer fate, and all those signs along the road have turned into answers, and all the answers say that I'm brighter now, better now. But if I take a closer look I can see that things are only brighter because I choose to believe them different. There's that, and the blinding frost over the outdoors.

It's a strange season in this part of town. People can't keep their balance here because there's an extra layer to the world, a

freeze that forces them to protect themselves with the capsiz-
ing bulk of coats and underwear and scarves. These protective
layers bind and weight the people, their limbs stiffen and their
movement slows until they're turned into blunted beings who
can do no harm. They're kind. I'd like to be like that too, but
the bus stops, and I don't have a chance to try any kindness
out, because everyone's leaving. I watch them exit and avoid
slippage by borrowing the safety of the footsteps stepped before them.

When my view is emptied of them I see a teenager waiting on a bench, a girl with red earmuffs. By the looks of her
swollen eyes, I'd say she's wearing those red earmuffs to keep
the secrets out while she waits for someone to arrive. The earmuffs aren't doing their job though, because her grief mimics
the speedy drip of a nearby icicle. I don't want to watch the
girl wait anymore, I don't want to see her disappointed or sad;
I blow heavy on the window so as to cover her face with a
patch of breath, which is to say, I do my best, and then I write
"cloud" in the breath-patch, the way you do when you want
something to be. Warm or right or nameful, a swift correction
on the usual, a fair imposition on the actual scheme of things.

I get out at my brother's school. I check the gymnasium, the
photo lab, smoker's hill. But I see only kids on ropes, portraits
forging out of darkness, threads of grey on a shabby horizon.
I go to the boy's bathroom. There's usually good information
in bathrooms and my brother spends a lot of time parting his
hair in them. But instead of my brother I find a mist in front
of the mirror. The mist is made of cologne. It smells of all the
algebra equations that were ever solved, and from its center a
hall monitor emerges. He's wearing the customary turtleneck
and badge, the whistle on a string.

"You belong in the women's," he says.

I decide not to argue this point with him. I just wave good-bye and try to put him and the swear words scrawled on the walls behind me. I have my own curses to attend to, but the monitor won't let me go so easy.

"Wait a minute—where's your bathroom pass?"

I point to the difficulties on my head.

"There was an urgency," I explain.

We grow closer so he can inspect my injury.

"What happened to your face?"

"Accident in gym. Hockey."

"We don't play hockey here."

"I mean. Swimming."

"I don't believe you," he says, and he polishes his whistle to maximize its shrill potential. "I don't think you're where you're supposed to be at all."

"I'm trying to get back there," I say, as I leave. "I've been trying a long time."

"Just making sure you don't get lost or anything," he says. He follows me out and fondles his whistle.

"I can find my own way," I say, but I can tell he doesn't have any faith in my sense of direction because he quickens his pace and I quicken mine and then he's running after me, his whistle reporting on the fact that there's no time to waste.

"I'm going to turn you in," he shouts, and now he's catching up to me, he's wending quick and gaining fast, past fire hydrants and substitute teachers and student body presidents. I lose him only by creeping down to the field where there's a procession fugueing on icy ground, their tassels swinging, their flags to the wind. The band's song is a practice for keeping time that releases cold banners of air as they march. They finger their valves, they key, they strain. There's my brother.

Over there, with his cap pulled low. He's making his clarinet bray about what it feels like to be solo. He's a natural at that, but when he sees me he skips a beat and that particular beat must be a great loss to the song, because the band makes the defeated noise that happens when tubas turn into flutes and triangles go on strike, and I'm thinking that there might be no stopping the spread of this ruin when the music teacher descends. His baton accuses my brother and his shout puts a visible chill into the air.

"You plan on getting better anytime soon, Miguel?"

My brother nods his head, clarinet attached.

"Let's get it right this time people," the music teacher orders.

And so the band goes on to keep time together, they ascend, descend, crescendo. The music provides an ample cover for me as I push towards my brother. I avoid the snares, dodge the mallets, trample into the thick of the reeds to tap my brother's shoulder. He squeaks out a shocked note. I tell him there'll be time to talk later, and I try to pull him away from the crowd.

"Just a minute," he says, and he raises a hand to me and counts the beats down on his fingers, one and two and three and four and then he hits another flat note before issuing his thoughts in a forceful and discordant tone.

"Go away. I know you're not my sister. You're just my mind making me think you're my sister because my mind is leaving me."

"It is me, I swear."

And then the pudgy flutist at my brother's right pipes up.

"What happened to your sister's forehead?"

"That's not funny Christopher," Moses says. "Not funny at all."

It's even less funny when I feel the crack of a baton on my shoulder, and the music teacher demands to know why I like making a mess of his song. I point to my brother, whose face is practicing naiveté.

"Miguel? Do you have business with this person?"

My brother removes the spit valve from his instrument and empties it on my foot.

"Let me think about it," he says.

"What's there to think about?" the teacher says. "Do you know this person or not?"

My brother takes a fresh reed from his pocket. He moistens it with his tongue. He moistens it for a long time. Then he starts to chew. And walk away. I try to walk with him, but he's one of those fast walkers, and I'm slowed by the fact that I have to stoop to pick up his clarinet a lot. It seems my brother likes to throw instruments into the snow during difficult times. Finally, I catch up with him.

"I have another message from Mom," I tell him. "She's waiting for us. She wants me to take you to her."

"I believe you're lying to me," he says through a mouthful of reed.

"I'm not lying," I say. "Not quite. Well, maybe about the message part. Maybe about the waiting part."

My brother swallows.

"You're lying," he says. "So you must be real. The you that I made up in my head wouldn't lie to me. The you that I made up would take me seriously as a person and not try to protect my feelings all the time."

"There'll be time for that later," I say.

And so we leave behind all that brassy fanfare at a high pitch. We leave as quickly as we can, but even as we leave we can hear the music teacher delivering the final word on this never-ending song.

"Okay, people," he says. "This is your last chance."

We go to my father's work. We look in the chapel, the supply closet, the ambulance. But we find only a kneeling of the
bereaved. Bouquets of crutches. Stretcherfuls of empty. We
go to the front desk where the receptionist smells her roses
and reads her cards. I knew her back when I worked here, back
when I was still giving it a go. She gets roses from every hurt
flirt, and there's a lot of hurt around here, so we have to crane
over the thorns to make our request.

"We need to see a nurse," my brother says.

"I can't imagine that there's anything wrong with you," the
receptionist winks.

"That might be true," Moses concedes. "But there is something wrong with her."

He pushes me forward and my face drips on the counter
as evidence.

"That's a nasty wound there," she says. "Where're your
stitches?"

"They got lost," I explain, "when I took them out and
threw them down a hole."

"We try to discourage that," the receptionist says. She
stares at us until a more scenic injury trots up, a gash in the
arm of a handsome and available man that enables us to trip
past the desk and through the hall. We pull back curtains and
open doors until we find Dad. He's tending to a cop with a
convention of sores on his arms. When Dad sees us, he drops
his bandages, but still manages a suave introduction.

"Officer, these are my children," he says. "Children," he
says, "this is the law."

The cop doesn't pay much attention because he's having a
conversation with a walkie-talkie about being on the lookout

for some inmate that escaped. The subject is presumed to be harmed and languorous, the walkie-talkie says. The cop and the walkie laugh at that together for awhile, and then the cop turns on his sores and itches them gladly.

"Don't scratch," I tell him. "You'll just make things worse."

"You look familiar," the cop says. He pushes his sunglasses to the top of his head so he can have an undimmed view of me.

"It's the family resemblance," Dad says, and he hurries a smile onto his face.

"It's more than that," the cop says. "Did you go to school with my daughter?"

"I think I did, yes."

"What grade are you in now?"

"Freshman."

"Look a little old for a freshman."

"They held me back. Really hard."

"That's too bad," the cop says. "You should pay more attention to school. If you don't pay more attention to school you end up in jail. Remember that."

"I hear some people in jail don't belong there," Moses says.

"That's what they say. But if they're not bad going in they're going to be bad enough after they've been there awhile, so what's done is done I guess."

I can see my brother's frown circumscribed in the lens of the officer's sunglasses.

"What's wrong with you?" he asks. "What's your problem anyway?"

Dad hushes my brother, but the officer casts an understanding look over us all.

"I don't mind telling them," he says, and he extends his bandaged arms towards us. "You kids can learn from my mistakes. Don't think you can ever get too old for chicken pox. You can get chicken pox always. They just call it shingles instead."

"That's not what I mean," my brother says. "I mean, how can you think—"

I tell the officer not to mind my brother, that he's just upset because of that person that's on the loose, the escapee. We think we might have seen her.

"Tell me everything you know," the cop says. He takes out a pad and writes intently, he writes all my words down, especially the ones about how we ran into a suspicious person in the lobby who was trying to corrupt us, to kidnap us, to hold us hostage to some great fiction in the world that sees no evil and he crosses the t's of what I'm saying, and then, he holds up his hand, he stops me.

"So you say this person had eyes like a domino? Haircut like a boiled owl? Lisp like an arrow in heat?"

"Yes."

"And her face looked like, in your words, a dirty mousetrap?"

"That's her. That's the culprit."

"Well," says the officer. "Well, well, well, I guess I'll have to look into it," and he smirks a thank you to Dad and shuffles out into the lobby. He carries his sticky arms stiff before him, like one of those men in the movies that walk in death for life. His walkie-talkie sounds off from his breast pocket. It says over.

I could argue about that. But I'm not sure I want to, because from what I can tell, that statement might be right. All the time I see people who are over and on their way out to an ending. They die better than most, because they can see it coming, and they run faster, because memory can only take you so far. Once they're at the end of themselves, people also discover talents that they never knew they had. I hear it's different for everyone. My father's talent might be handstands, and my brother's might be girls or comics or amoeba-watching. I'm not sure. I can only be sure of my mother's talent since I saw it long ago, back when I was a baby who had to look up, stare up, always, because I lived on a patch of tile in the bathroom. I had a great point of view, but it hurt when my mother showed me her talent because the heel of her dance shoe pierced my hand. I was too busy watching her dance to get her out of the way. I couldn't move. That was my talent, I thought.

When the officer is gone Dad takes us both by our collars and leads us into the parking lot. His hands tremble as he opens the doors for us. Then he closes the doors and sits down and clenches the steering wheel. I take a long look at the new flap of age at his jaw, a stubbled little annex that no tidy measure of beard can hide.

"Did I make you older?" I ask.

"Yes," Dad says.

"I'm sorry."

"It was going to happen anyway."

"How many years are we talking here?"

"If you're thinking about trying to pay me back," he says, "don't."

Which is kind of him. I'm not even sure how much I owe Dad, but I think it's more than I can afford. His grey alone could ruin me. Still, there are things I can try.

"What if I got Mom back? I know where she is. What if I did that?"

Dad looks away from me, which is comforting, and familiar. He's always looked away from me while acknowledging the possibilities of my person. It's a given reflex in our familial nature, like loving people when you don't want to, or removing splinters for fun. And then he looks at my forehead, and claps me on the shoulder.

"You think you can get your mother back?"

"Sure. What do you think this is all about anyway?"

He might not be saying much but I can tell that my father has a lot on his mind. Like my mother's face, and a fair fraction of her legs. I can tell what's on his mind because he's conducting a study of himself in the mirror, the kind of assessment that's necessary only when you're about to be reunited with the one who left you. He surveys the eye-slope and the forehead-shuffle, but my brother interrupts before he gets around to the premature meander at his hairline.

"What do we do now?" Moses asks.

"First," Dad says. "I'm going to take a moment."

So we sit and watch nothing happen through the window when a girl ambles by with balloons that instruct sick people to shed their sufferings. Dad lowers his head onto the steering wheel at the sight of them. The horn goes off. Its blare startles one of the balloons to a pop, and this heavenly death moves Dad into action.

"First, let's be safe," he says. "Buckle your seatbelts kids."

He tries to snap his belt across his chest but the belt snaps back. He fights with the clasp, wheedles it towards the buckle, gives up, and pretends that we don't notice.

"Second, I'm going to ask Moses-Miguel to play a little music because a little music is something I could use right now."

My brother hits all the wrong notes. I know the repentant tune he attempts. It should lilt and steeple, but it brawls and honks. At least you can't hear Dad grinding his teeth over the music though, at least there's that.

"Now," Dad says. "We're going to go to the diner and pick up some protein. We need to keep our strength up."

"Can I get a popsicle instead?" I ask.

"No," Dad says, and he herds me tight to him. "Sugar isn't good for you. I only want what's good for you. You understand?"

I think he yelled that last part at me. I'm pretty sure he did because my ear is ringing in tribute to an alarming loss.

"And after that?" Moses asks.

"After that we turn her in," he says, and his voice trails off because he's already practicing for the dissolve of our attachments. I can't blame him. Dad always likes to be prepared, even if it's only for the dangle of unexpected turns. Moses is less understanding.

"I don't believe you," he says.

"Believe me," Dad says. "We're turning her in, but we're going to have to take a different route to the authorities because this scenery does nothing for my nerves and since your mother is somewhere along the way we might as well stop in and say hello to the one-that-got-away-again-and-again-and-again. Now who's got the map? Does anyone even know where we're going?"

My thoughts say they know where we're going. They try to talk me out of it because I'm not up for that kind of downfall, and when I don't listen they pretend they don't know me. They claim they're not my thoughts at all, just sensations on hugging terms with the dust. But I'd know my thoughts anywhere.

Mostly, they want to know what talent is going to be found at the end of me. To be honest, I'm hoping for something in the way of throwing my voice. I've always wanted to pitch it, just to see it speak from a spot where it can be put to better use. It'd be nice if my voice was a laugh for anyone who'd have it, a mutt dog or a tightrope walker, maybe a nimbus. Anyone like and unlike me: someone who never began, someone who always wanted to. I'm not picky. And if my stammer can't perform an inch of good, then maybe it can just sound off for the loneliness that comes when you least expect it. And in that case, my voice will be a hum.

When we arrive, it's curtains. A drapery of blue, their pleats cupping ticket stubs and ash. The theatre lobby smells of damp cards and trapdoors and grease paint, and the reek gains ground the closer we get to the ticket booth that houses a bowl of goldfish and a tuxedoed usher who looks to be six, maybe seven years old. He doesn't see us at first, because he's occupied with feeding the goldfish and helping himself to their flakes. For every pinch the fish get, he takes three for himself. Which seems fair enough, because a person can't make a living at a place like this. He's dedicated to his duties, pausing only to struggle with a bottle of aspirin. Frustrated by its childproof qualities, he rolls his eyes, and one of their rotations captures my family in a glance. He regards us skeptically, his eyes narrowing under the wayward drag of a young comb-over.

"This is where the magic happens," he says in greeting, and then he resumes the application of pointy teeth to the bottle cap.

"We need to get in there," my brother tells him.

"You're too late. It's almost over," the usher says.

We don't move.

"I'd like to help you people," the usher says. "You seem nice. Remind me of my own family. But I can't disturb the show. We got beasts in there. Animals too. And if you're not there at the beginning the end could be dangerous. You might not understand."

"We're looking for someone who works here," Dad says.

"Is it me?" the usher asks with a hopeful tug at his bowtie.

"No," I say.

"Well then," the usher says, and he goes back to struggling with his aspirin bottle. "Well now," he says.

"Got a headache?" Dad asks.

The usher shakes the bottle at him in answer. The rattle tells of an insistent pang that moves my father to roll up his sleeves. The usher opens the door to his booth and Dad steps inside to get a closer look at this painful situation.

"I'm a nurse you see," Dad says. "I could open that bottle for you. But that's a temporary fix. It's better to find out what's really wrong. Now tell me, how do you take care of yourself?"

The usher motions to the airless booth and the goldfish going belly-up.

"This is my life," he says.

"Seems stressful," Dad notes. "Maybe you should loosen that tie of yours. It might be cutting off some of your air."

"I never thought of that."

"And how much sleep do you get?"

"There's a lot to do around here," the usher says. "I have to make the brass shine so I can count my freckles in it, and I have hundreds of freckles. One for every event that goes wrong. And we have a lot of wrong events around here—"

The usher buries his face in Dad's pant leg. He has a large collection of woe to articulate into the khaki, and the whimper

of his comb-over indicates that this might take awhile. My father gestures for us to go on without him. I argue that we'll
wait. I argue by not moving my feet. If I leave him again, he
might go so grey that I won't recognize him anymore and not
recognizing my father isn't something I'm willing to do while
I'm still around. I'd always hoped that when it came down to it,
my father would be doing a handstand while I threw my voice.
We'll wait, I insist, and then I see my feet begin to heel and toe
across the carpet because my brother is dragging me forward,
and then he pushes me through the doors, into a dark of boo
and hiss.

All that rots is rotting here. In this darkness there's a raised
stink, a quiver of applause, a fray of children unraveling in
hopes of an encore. Here, cakes fly with doves. The ceiling
sheds feathers and frosting. I wipe the sugar from my eye, blow
the down from my arm. The show isn't going as planned, un-
less the show is supposed to be a belch of seethe and a welter
of murk. If that's the case, then everything's fine.

"Where are you?" my brother asks. Already, we've lost each
other.

"Over here."

"You mean—here?"

A low voice fumbles out a growl. It says that the lost
shouldn't put their hands where they don't belong. The lost
hand, it explains, should stick to cutting itself off when it gets
too fingery.

"We're not lost," I point out. And then I yell to my brother.
"Over here."

I've heard that this place has the best shadows in town. I
have my doubts. There's hardly a light to cause a shadow here,
and the dim has left everyone wandering.

"There you are," I hear my brother say, even though he's nowhere near, and he must've mistaken me for someone else and clutched a strange shoulder because another voice pipes up. It says that feels bad. It says, a little to the left. It says that a bad feeling shouldn't go to waste just because you're too good to know it's happening.

"We know it's happening," I argue.

These voices sound familiar but they don't belong to me. I'm sure of it, because you can't throw anything, not even a voice, without knowing the loss of what was held, even if it was just an oath of silence on the back of a goodbye. I don't feel the whole of that loss yet, just the parts that interlude and curdle, so I figure that the voices are just jokes that belong to my brother. I turn to tell Moses that I'm on to him, and that's when I see that he's had no time for jokes because he's too concerned with the guidance of his own feet. Our shoes cling to the floor by strands of a violent bubblegum; we trip and stumble and steady ourselves against the velvet backs of chairs.

"Do you know what you're going to say to her?" he asks.

"I've practiced."

"What do you think she'll say back?"

"I practiced that too," I say. "But probably not enough."

We follow footfalls that instruct us to follow their sticky lead until they stop and it comes to our attention that there are some stranded children blocking the way. They're trying to cross a body of water in the aisle, this lake of a puddle adrift, its marine aspect due to pipe bursts and roof leaks and the sad state of things as overseen by a careless management. The children clothe the puddle with coats, their flesh reinventing the goosebump as they venture across the aisle, one pair of legs and then another, their steps making like stones across the water. There's a teenaged opportunist who's appointed himself in charge, and he collects clothing as a toll. My brother offers up his jacket. I hand over my socks.

"Holes won't get you anywhere," says the toll-taker.

It occurs to me that there must be another way to get by. Some shortcut or alternative route. But I've been going the other way for too long, and for once, I'd like to pass the way other people do. As a person or a girl. Less scrap, more some-one. The best option being someone along the steady lines of my brother, whose hands are already full with a solution.

"Here," he says, and he pays my way with the sweater that his foster knit. It's a nostalgic addition to the puddle, and its stripes are helpful in keeping us in line as we cross. There's a push of kids before us and a pull of them behind, they're jittered with anticipation and funned up with haste, but my brother and I manage to stay out of trouble until I stumble into some, accidentally, by pulling a braid of hair. I don't mean any harm. It's just that this gold braid springs like a handle from the head of the girl in front of me, and I need something to hold onto. Its owner turns to me, her cheek striped with cake sugar. She snaps at me to stop, so I smile, and then she sees that I can't mean any harm because I have no teeth, and her face goes plush with query. She wants to know if I've seen anyone that she might belong to. She says that if I have, I don't even have to tell her out loud. She says I can just yank her hair twice. Just two yanks, and then she'll know. When I let go of her braid she starts to weep.

It's not so bad as that, I say.

"As bad as what?" she wants to know.

As bad as never, I want to say. As bad as always. But I can't say anything because I don't have the answers. Which doesn't seem to matter much to her. I've noticed that people don't expect answers when they look at me anymore, just questions and games and the makings of each. This gold girl is no exception. She wipes her tears, pulls a red handkerchief from her nostril, and suggests a diversion.

"Pin the tail," she says, and she brandishes a papery curlicue.

But I don't see any donkeys. There's only a cluster of kids staring at me wantingly, the glint in their eyes matched only by the silver points of tacks in their palms. They clutch paper tails in their hands, ready to perform the blindfolded spin that precedes a stab in the dark. My brother nods warily at this crowd and pushes me forward.

"We should keep going," he says to them. "We'll be late for our mother."

The kids look ashamed of themselves after hearing about our plans. They put their hands in their pockets so as to forget what they've done, but not everyone here is gifted with the resources to conceal their guilt. Those without pockets resort to other measures. They try to hide the donkey tails beneath their shirts, nearest their belly buttons, but the curlicues won't be hidden. They poke and spiral like new starts, and I hear the kids reason that these coiled facsimiles of umbilical beginnings prove that they were not born, but they were made.

I knew that reasoning, once.

It's not getting any better in here, but at least it's brighter for us now. There's a brief break in the dark because there's a thin boy building a thinner fire in the middle of the aisle, his kid-skin flush with heat, his kid-shadow cast in a kindled light. It's a revealing little pile of flame, not because of the light it leaks, but because the small body it toasts tells us what we've missed. From the looks of it, that rabbit's been out of the hat

for some time. Now its only concern is the spit, where it's occupied with the trick of turning from white to black. The kid
tries not to look his dinner in the face, focusing instead on the
fret of sparks in the air.

"I guess you have to keep your strength up somehow," my
brother reassures him.

The kid nods and feeds the fire with a handful of candles,
celebratory tapers of the type that won't be blown out, but can
only be extinguished with water. He's so happy tossing wicks
that I hate to interrupt him, but I have to know if he's seen
our mother.

"She's this skinny," I say. "And that shaky."

"I can't say," the boy says. "I don't know that many mothers."

There's a tracery of deception in his voice, but I figure he
must have a reason, even if it's just that I can't afford the privileged information of these backwards parts.

"We should really keep going anyway," my brother says.

We start to walk away from this flammable site, my brother
and I, but we don't get very far before the kid cries out because
he's been sitting with the ashes too much. First we see a spark
sucking on his toe and I suggest we blow it out and then the
spark starts to lick his ankle and my brother explains that it's
probably too late for air, we might want to consider water at
this point, and the kid keeps piping up, he says he wishes he
knew the word for this feeling. He'd like to say that it stings,
but it's more than that somehow. My brother fails to supply the
needed term, but he snuffs out the burn with his hand, and his
face indicates that he isn't comfortable leaving an injury out
like this, open to onlookers and ready for infection. He looks
at the kid, and then he looks at me.

"I'll catch up to you later," he says, but he doesn't sound

so sure, and this is a cause for happiness on my part, even if it isn't so much happiness as it is a decision to act like I am, because my brother has always had to set an example for me and I don't want him to think that it wasn't a good one, a happy one. My brother and I will always have his goodness, I tell myself, and I leave him only because leaving means that I can move closer to what we're both so afraid of. Even if it just looks like a stage where there's just a card walking on edge, an ace afoot, its diamonds on tiptoe.

I've seen it all except for certain sights on my long walk through the theatre. By the time the aisle becomes the front row I've seen a worm enter the hide of an apple and exit as an arrow. I've witnessed milk sour into love letters and fleas scamper in formation. A blue telephone rang and laid an egg. A needle in a stack of needles turned into a strand of hay, a veil danced with a plume of steam, a cherry stem performed a backbend.

"Did I miss the big act?" I ask the girl in the front row, a clap-happy soul with a droopy party hat.

"It's still coming," she says, patting the seat beside her. It's occupied by a triangle of cake, a spongy leftover that'd love to spite my stomach with its violet innards and layered gloam. I bite before it can bite me first. I know that's how it often goes, but there's no satisfaction as I swallow, just a new hunger that mingles with my insides and sets my hands to a high tremble.

And then the curtain parts and a magician takes a rickety bow. He's a spit-shined old character, and the bony flourish of his entrance leaves him bent in half so that the sad spectacle of his eyes are fixed on the floor while he speaks.

"What you're about to see is really something," he says.

The stage remains empty, the creak of the old man's cough its only substitute for a performance. It's not as entertaining as it could be, but I have to give the cough credit for trying. The rest of the audience isn't as forgiving, they have higher expectations than I do, and they demonstrate their impatience with the cooperation of their most spankable regions. They bare and wag. This isn't what they came for.

"Just a minute," sighs the magician. Careful to avoid eye contact with the wagging crowd, he rights his suited form with a crack and calls for curtains. They drape on command and provide ample cover for his ancient self, but they can't conceal the whispered reprimands, the coax and the shuffle, all the old entreaties to pull it together, just this once, just this last time.

Someone is missing their cue. This isn't what I came for either.

But then the curtains open on a woman who isn't ready for this kind of magic. She's too busy fussing with a hive of hair, a teased keeper of snarls and knots that shelters all the homeless, the bees and the bobby pins, the leaves and the moths. That hairdo is rooted in charitable principles, and it's not for a lack of welcome that a mouse finds itself falling out of the curls. The audience laughs at its furry tumble. The woman tries to act like she's laughing too, but I've seen that kind of shake before, and judging by its tremor I wouldn't place bets on a real laugh chancing by anytime soon. There's that, and the fact that I can see the hesitation of a tear in her eyelash. She tries to cry into a tissue but the tissue keeps shredding into doves and the tears themselves just wait in the wings of her lashes, so she gives up on feeling anything, she goes still, goes quiet, and is moved only when a thrust occurs at the curtain's edge.

A cane pokes at her nethered cheeks, the bottommost of her person, a pinched rear mounted in black leotard. The woman responds to this poke by summoning a matchbook from her hair and lighting a cigarette, leaving the magician with no choice but to rap harder on her thigh-backs. Pained, the woman emits a smoky squeal. The squeal sounds like it's been assembled over many years in her throat, built with whisper-scraps and mumbled protests and thoughts that never held the status of a word. The squeal is familiar to me, and I want the cane to hit the woman some more so I can hear it again. Maybe if I could hear the squeal again I would know who the woman is for sure.

But I'm not lucky enough to hear that spangled sound again, because instead of squealing the woman hits the cane back. She grasps it with both hands and pulls. She plants her patent heels on the stage and tugs, but the cane's too wily for her. It escapes her fingers and strikes her twice on each flank. The woman can handle the blows, but her stockings can't, they rend on the run and expose her bruises for the purple snitches that they are. She hitches up the stockings and tries to talk them into standing by her, if only for the sake of appearances. Even though her act doesn't mean much, she says, she'd like a decent appearance, or maybe even an upright one, but the cane has other ideas, and letting the woman appear upright isn't one of them. It upsets her with a blow. The woman falls and I start to wonder if that's it, if that's all, but then she picks herself up and tries to walk, and for a minute or so, the walk works. She walks like she learned how to walk underwater. She walks like she has no need of air, with feet that can't recognize the ground and hands that aren't aware of the troublesome solidity of being. It's a glide of a walk, a real sidle in charm, and the magician looks pleased until she adds an outstretched palm to her approach.

"After," the magician hisses, and he issues another rap. "You get paid after. Keep your head up. Don't stand so funny."

The woman thrusts her chin in the air. Bones caper in her cheeks. She glances at her feet and organizes them toe to toe.

"Now give us a smile."

The woman licks her lips and squints, her dimples smirking out in full. They're the best holes in the face that a person could ever have. Especially when that person is the mother of me, as this person is, as I now recognize her to be.

"Keep smiling," the magician whispers, but my mother droops instead. The magician tries to straighten her. He clutches her shoulders, pinches her ribs, chokes her waist to attention. And then he gives up and props her spindled frame against the long box that's waiting for her onstage. I wave at her. I can tell that she sees me because she's smiling back like that, she's smiling that smile that says: I know you from somewhere. I'm just not sure who you are. Are you the real entertainment? The cause of my crossed fingers? The sight that split my side? Are you some kind of prize, a source of sickness, my favorite friend? Are you the one that was made from me to prove a sad point? Who owes who? Do we have some kind of arrangement, you and I?

I figure the woman deserves a hint, so I show her the plank of my tongue, which I still carry by way of identification. At first, I'm afraid she won't recognize it. My tongue isn't what it used to be. It's violet from cake sugar, and has developed a taste for cures at the point of the knife. But my mother must see the stutter on its buds because her dimples deepen with realization, and her smile says: I know you, you're the one from the busted bed, the one who jumped so high that the bed croaked and kicked the bucket that caught the leak in the ceiling, but you kept jumping and I just laid there, watching you, I watched you go up and down and mostly up and eventually I left because that's how I wanted to remember you. Mostly up.

Up there, midair, nearest the light bulb, your fingertip dusty where it stroked the moths gathered there. Yes, that's it, my mother's smile says, and then it dwindles to a vanish. Whether it vanishes because there's nothing left to say or because it can't say for certain I don't know, and maybe I'll never know, because she's disappearing from me again, piece by piece, she's parceling her limbs into a contained darkness.

"Now," says the magician to the audience. "This is the trick."

And so we see my mother lowering her person into the box. It holds her tight. Except for her head and its hairdo, except for her legs and their clackety shoes. These spare parts dangle from holes outside her boxed body. Between pearly gloves the magician displays a saw, a polished wake of divide and cut that makes the audience gasp. We witness our reflections in it, the saw, watch our faces change to metallic faces in its surface. The magician pricks a gloved thumb on the saw to prove its sharpness with a lethargic drop of blood, and then he knocks on the box so we can hear the honest echo of my mother's bones connecting to one another.

Her bones don't sound much different than my own. Now I know you, they say, now I don't. I crack my knuckles in response. But that doesn't change anything. The magician still saws, he still makes the blade gnash and portion until the box achieves a separation and parts ways so that where my mother's togetherness once was there's just a distance that allows her to go on living in pieces. She clicks her heels together from one end of her existence and nods her head from the other.

"She can't feel a thing," the magician announces.

The audience bobs their party hats with approval, but I don't enjoy this estrangement. I climb onstage to reach her but the curtain falls on my neck, and I see the magician in the wings, but he's too busy applying a band-aid over his gloved thumb to help me. I try to lift the curtain but the curtain won't lift, so I crawl beneath it and cross the stage and in the spot where my mother's halves once writhed, so white and lively in their severance, is a whiskered token of softness. The mouse sniffs at my feet and employs a shudder as a symbol of its fear. It senses the desperate thoughts on me, it knows that I've become so small that I'd trample it to get what I want, and it probably wouldn't mind that so much if either of us believed that being underfoot meant that we might be able to crawl without giving chase to some animal still lesser than ourselves. But the least of creatures is best off on the long, long run. So the mouse does. So it runs. Its heels scurry, its toes scram, its tail flags; I follow the tail and something starts to drift, at first I think it's me, but then I see that it's only snow. The snowflakes blank and I follow the mouse-tail through their flurry, this pale way, that pale way, till I'm following white on white into the banks and I can't see the mouse anymore because I'm looking at a door. Behind the door I hear a hum, a hum I know well, since it's in a voice specific to my throat. The humming stops. I hear a shuffling at the door, and the sound of an ear brooding against the woodgrain.

"What can you do for me?" she asks.

"I'll make you like me," I say. "I'll make you like me so much that soon you'll start telling me you love me, over and over, and you'll say that this is just another day for me, that I can do it all over again, all the going on, somehow on, anyhow on, and I'll probably never believe you but I want to try."

At the peephole an eye appears. The doorknob turns.

"Come in," my mother says.